AGENTS OF DECEPTION

A COLLECTION OF SHORT THRILLERS

SAM CHASE

First Edition

Editing by Jessica McKenna
Cover by Sam Chase

BEACHES AND TRAILS
PUBLISHING

ALLIANCE

A SHORT THRILLER

CHAPTER 1
COUNTDOWN TO CRISIS

JACK JONES MOVED QUICKLY through the concrete corridors beneath the launch facility, his every step shadowed by the rhythmic blare of alarms echoing down the dim hallways. The missile countdown had begun, and he only had minutes to disable the warhead buried somewhere below ground in this web of tunnels. His handler's voice crackled through his earpiece.

"Jack, we're running out of time," Director Gene Farrow's tone was calm but edged with urgency. "If the missile launches, it's an international crisis."

"Almost there." Jack's voice was as steady as his hands, though every nerve hummed with the weight of his mission. He rounded a corner, pressing his back to the damp wall as he scanned the corridor ahead. The missile room was close—too close to mess up now.

A door marked RESTRICTED ACCESS loomed at the end of the corridor. Jack's heartbeat ticked up as he hacked the entry panel, watching the red light blink as his device worked to override security. In seconds, the door slid open with a hiss, and he slipped inside, ducking behind a row of control panels.

The missile sat in the center of the room, a chilling figure cast in cold steel. Clusters of wires and sensors around its base broke its sleek lines only. Jack pulled out his tools and knelt beside the device, forcing himself to focus past the heat and sweat running into his eyes.

"Jack, we're down to two minutes. Are you in?" Farrow's voice sounded again, the calm unraveling.

"Working on it," Jack muttered, tearing open the missile's control panel. Inside, wires lay in a twisted snarl, their vibrant colors taunting him with deadly options. One wrong choice, and the missile would launch, taking half of London with it.

He held his breath, blinking away sweat. Come on, Jones. Focus.

Finally, he found the wire he hoped was the one. With a deep breath, he cut it.

The timer's relentless beeping fell silent, the last seconds frozen in a quiet, unblinking red. Jack exhaled slowly, calm flooding him. "Bomb's neutralized. Missile's dead."

"You're clear to evacuate," Farrow said. "Extraction's waiting at the east exit. Move now."

Jack turned to leave, adrenaline giving way to relief—until he heard footsteps echoing down the corridor. Not just one set—multiple.

Two guards in tactical gear rounded the corner, weapons already raised. Jack dropped low as a hail of bullets shattered the silence. He rolled across the concrete, firing two shots that both hit their marks. The guards slumped to the floor, and Jack rose, ready to sprint for the staircase.

But before he reached it, a third figure blocked his path—a woman with red hair and striking green eyes, her pistol aimed squarely at his chest.

"Agent Jones." Her voice sliced through the tense silence, sharp and precise.

Jack's eyes narrowed. "Can't say I recognize you. Or is this one of those anonymous favors?"

Her expression remained ice-cold. "Agent Jack Jones, American. NESA. This facility is under EISA's protection. You're interfering in a classified European operation."

Jack's jaw tightened. "Noted. But I'm here under NESA orders, not for diplomacy."

Her eyes flickered with impatience. "You've already tripped three of our sensors, Jones. I'm here to contain this breach before it reaches Isaac's syndicate. Cooperate, or your interference becomes a risk we'll need to… mitigate."

"Cooperate?" Jack flashed a dry smile, his hand inching toward his weapon. "EISA doesn't have the clearance. Or the authority."

Her gaze hardened, voice dropping a notch colder. "Your director will be hearing from mine. Step back. EISA has jurisdiction here, and I'll finish what you started."

Jack's stance remained locked, neither of them willing to yield. The air between them buzzed with distrust, two agents as immovable as the steel missile looming behind them.

In a blur, she closed the distance, twisting his arm and forcing him against the wall. His gun clattered to the floor as he clenched his teeth against the pain radiating up his arm.

"Still want an introduction?" she asked, her face mere inches from his. "Name's Irina Stepanov. And I'm your worst nightmare if you don't get out of my way."

Jack grunted, twisting out of her grip and stepping back, his stance solid. Irina's pistol was again trained on his chest, her gaze a cold warning.

"You think you can intimidate me?" Jack's voice was low, daring. "I've met people with plenty of scary names, and most of them are dead."

She arched a brow. "Let me guess—you're the one who killed them?"

Jack gave her a mocking salute. "Right on."

Irina's lips tightened as she moved to circle him, each step calculated. Jack mirrored her movements, his eyes never leaving hers, the tension between them like a live wire.

Finally, she broke the silence. "Take the east exit. My team has control of the facility now. Whatever intel you collected is irrelevant."

"Is that so?" Jack let his hand drift to his backup pistol. "I thought EISA and NESA were on the same side."

She scoffed, tone clipped. "This mission was EISA's alone. If your director forgot to brief you, it's not my problem."

Farrow's voice buzzed faintly in Jack's ear, but he tuned it out, keeping his focus on Irina. "Who's running this operation? Isaac?"

For the first time, her confidence flickered, but she quickly masked it, her expression hardening. "I don't answer to you, Jones. Leave now, and there doesn't have to be any bloodshed."

His grip tightened on his pistol as he measured his options, every instinct screaming that there was more to this woman than she let on. But before he could respond, footsteps echoed from the corridor behind him. Jack turned, glimpsing three more figures moving toward them.

"Friends of yours?" he asked, turning back to Irina—but she was already moving, slipping past him with practiced agility, vanishing into the shadows.

Jack gritted his teeth. He'd lost too much time already. Without another glance back, he sprinted toward the east exit, his footsteps echoing through the cold, dark tunnels.

He emerged into the open air as helicopter blades sliced through the night sky. Farrow's voice crackled in his ear, "Jones, what happened in there? You were radio silent."

Jack looked back at the facility, where the last shadows of Irina and her team disappeared into the darkness. "Just a little... international cooperation."

"Get in the chopper. We've got a debrief waiting." Farrow's tone was clipped, but Jack knew he'd have questions.

"Copy that," Jack replied, climbing into the helicopter as it ascended.

As the city lights dwindled below, his mind lingered on the woman who'd appeared out of nowhere. EISA, Russian, sharp, and dangerous —Irina Stepanov.

And he had a feeling this wouldn't be the last time they crossed paths.

CHAPTER 2
UNEASY ALLIANCES

THE NEXT EVENING, Jack sat in the National Essential Security Agency's debrief room, the low hum of the overhead lights blending with the hiss of the air conditioner. He'd barely closed his eyes since his run-in with Irina Stepanov, and her interference gnawed at him. The look she'd given him had been as icy as it was guarded. Just who was she really working for?

Director Gene Farrow entered the room, his expression grim. He set a thin dossier on the table and slid it toward Jack.

"Good work at the launch facility," Farrow said, his gaze assessing. "You kept a disaster from hitting the world stage. But now we've got bigger problems."

Jack opened the file and scanned the top page. A glossy headshot of a young man with blond hair and a carefully calculated look of detachment stared back.

"Dimitri Mirek Fedorov," Farrow continued. "He's an up-and-coming fashion designer—headline shows, magazines, the works. But his 'career' isn't all glitz. We suspect he's a key informant for a Russian syndicate that moves information and resources across Europe, Asia, and back to New York."

Jack raised an eyebrow. "The Russian mob's got a fashion consultant?"

Farrow's mouth tightened, almost a smile. "Not quite. Fedorov's been Isaac's courier for years, slipping in and out of elite circles across Paris, Milan, New York. He's dodged Interpol, evade our radar, and make powerful connections—all under the guise of designer shows. By day, he's an innocent tastemaker; by night, he's Isaac's middleman."

Jack tapped the photo. "And the objective? Surveillance or extraction?"

Farrow's gaze hardened. "We need him alive—and talking. Dimitri is our best link to Isaac Denisovich, head of a syndicate running assassinations, smuggling, arms trafficking across continents. Isaac's network is entrenched in every major port from Paris to Shanghai. If Dimitri leads us to him, we'll be closer than ever to dismantling the operation."

Jack nodded, taking it in. "What about EISA? They'll expect us to share our intel on Isaac."

Farrow's expression darkened. "Let's just say EISA's presence isn't optional. They'll be watching, and so will you. Stay close to Dimitri, but keep a low profile. If Isaac's people sense a threat, we're dead in the water."

Jack slipped the photo back into the file. "Understood. I'll keep my focus on Dimitri—and EISA's presence minimal."

Farrow's nod was brisk. "This is our best shot at getting to Isaac. Don't miss it."

Jack's eyes narrowed. "You're certain about Dimitri? This could be another dead-end."

"Possibly," Farrow admitted, "but he's surrounded himself with people who match profiles of wanted agents and spies. And there's more." Farrow's gaze turned unreadable. "EISA's suddenly taken an interest in him, running a parallel investigation. Supposedly after the same network."

The mention of EISA set off alarms in Jack's mind. He leaned back, crossing his arms. "This wouldn't have anything to do with Irina Stepanov, would it?"

Farrow's eyes glinted. "So, you met her. I thought it'd take EISA about a day to send their best agent into this operation."

"Is that what they call her?" Jack's tone sharpened. "She nearly compromised my mission. She's running her own agenda—sounds like turf war, not 'international cooperation.'"

Farrow's expression turned steely. "Watch her closely, Jack. EISA's been stepping into American operations more often lately, and we believe Isaac has someone inside their ranks. It's very possible Stepanov's involvement is... complicated."

Jack raised a brow. "You think she's in Isaac's pocket?"

"Possibly. Or she's playing her own game. Either way, keep an eye on her. But remember, your priority is Dimitri. We'll be tracking and supporting you on-site, but once you're in, you're alone."

"Understood." Jack glanced back at the file, committing Dimitri's face and the mission brief to memory. His instincts were already calculating scenarios and angles to gain Dimitri's trust.

Farrow added, "You'll have backup in case things escalate."

"Who?"

The door opened, and Jack's eyes narrowed as Irina Stepanov entered, cool and composed as ever. She crossed her arms, her gaze steely and unreadable.

"Agent Stepanov will join you," Farrow said, ignoring Jack's reaction. "Consider it a cooperative effort between NESA and EISA."

Jack suppressed a wry smile. "Cooperative? That's... optimistic."

Irina merely raised an eyebrow. "Try to keep up, Agent Jones."

Farrow continued, voice firm. "Dimitri will be in New York for his upcoming fashion show. It's the perfect chance to make contact. Agent Stepanov will be his 'escort'—you'll be her partner, posing as her date."

Jack felt irritation flare, but kept his tone neutral. "I'm the plus-one?"

Irina's lips quirked in a subtle smirk. "I'll handle introductions. You just need to look the part."

Before Jack could respond, Farrow raised a hand. "This is your mission, Jack. Stay focused. Professional. This isn't about EISA or Stepanov. Get the intel and don't let anything cloud your judgment."

Jack bit back a retort. He nodded. "Understood."

Farrow nodded approvingly. "Good. You'll leave tonight. Make it count."

Later That Night

Hours later, Jack found himself on the arm of Irina Stepanov as they entered the grand ballroom of New York's Savoy Hotel. Models drifted down a mirrored runway beneath chandeliers, the reflections scattering across the crowd like shards of glass.

Jack's gaze swept the room, his attention tuned to every threat, every stranger who might work for Isaac. The event felt too exposed, and he couldn't shake a sense of unease. His attention flicked to Irina, who moved seamlessly, her eyes locked on their target. Jack studied her, analyzing each glance and shift of her gaze.

Memories surfaced—fieldwork with NESA, alliances ending in betrayal. Trust had become a scarce currency in Jack's life, especially among agents like Irina. The thought gnawed at him that maybe EISA had inserted her here for their own purposes. He clenched his jaw. This mission was about staying ahead of Isaac, not weighing every move Irina made.

"There." Irina inclined her head toward a group gathered near the runway. Dimitri stood at the center, his sharp blue suit as impeccable as his reputation.

He spoke animatedly, gesturing as he laughed. But even from a distance, Jack noticed a flicker of something guarded in Dimitri's eyes, an edge beneath the charm.

"What's the move?" Jack murmured.

Irina's smile didn't falter. "Stay close. He knows me, not you."

They stopped a few feet from Dimitri, waiting. Jack eased into the background as Irina raised a hand. Dimitri spotted her, a flicker of recognition and surprise lighting his face.

"Irina! A pleasure to see you," Dimitri greeted her, his accent smooth and precise.

"Dimitri." Irina's smile was flawless as she took his hand. "It's been too long. Let me introduce my partner." She gestured to Jack. "This is Jack—he's very interested in learning more about your work."

Jack extended his hand, expression neutral. "Impressive designs. Your versatility is… something."

Dimitri's eyes flashed with suspicion, but he shook Jack's hand with a polite nod. "Ah, versatility—high praise from a man of taste. But what kind of man appreciates fashion?"

"Oh, just a man with an eye for elegance and… functionality," Jack replied, letting his gaze flick briefly to Irina. "Fascinated by how adaptable it all is."

Dimitri's smile remained, but his eyes sharpened. "Fashion is about expression. About identity."

"Speaking of," Irina cut in smoothly, "do you have time to catch up? I'd love to hear about your latest creations—and your travels."

Dimitri hesitated, a flicker of wariness in his gaze. "I might free up some time."

"Perfect," Irina said, her tone light but firm. "We'll be here. Enjoy the show."

As Dimitri excused himself, Jack and Irina shared a glance, both of them tense.

"He knows," Jack murmured. "Not the easiest mark."

Irina's gaze followed Dimitri, her expression unreadable. "Good. Cautious people slip up eventually."

Jack shot her a look. "You've done this before."

"Several times." She returned his gaze, a spark of challenge in her eyes. "Just remember—this is my mission. Don't get in my way."

The fashion show carried on, but Jack's attention split—half on Dimitri's disappearing form and half on Irina, her motives as layered and elusive as the evening itself.

CHAPTER 3
HIGH STAKES AT THE RUNWAY

JACK LEANED against a marble column at the edge of the Savoy's ballroom, his gaze steady on Dimitri as the young designer moved through the crowd. Dimitri's movements were polished but cautious; he shook hands, flash his award-winning smile, and cast frequent glances over his shoulder, as if expecting a shadow to follow him.

Irina approached, her expression unreadable as she handed Jack a glass of champagne. "Enjoying the view?"

Jack took the glass, keeping his voice low. "Dimitri's got more on his mind than fashion tonight."

Irina's eyes remained trained on their target. "He should. Our intel says he's planning to slip out early. I've arranged a car for us to follow."

Jack raised an eyebrow. "Didn't peg you for the chauffeur type."

Her lips curled faintly. "Try not to distract me, Jones."

The ballroom lights dimmed as the show's finale began, the crowd turning to watch the runway. Jack used the shift to keep an eye on Dimitri, who excused himself and disappeared through a side door.

Irina noticed, too. "Showtime."

They moved quickly, weaving through the oblivious crowd to the same door. Jack's hand drifted near the pistol under his jacket, his senses keyed up. This wasn't just another job; it was their best shot at finding someone close to Isaac's circle. If Dimitri led them to Isaac, the stakes would only climb from here.

Outside the ballroom, they entered a quiet hallway lined with gilt-framed paintings. Dimitri was already halfway to the end, his steps brisk.

Irina glanced at Jack. "Keep a bit of distance. No need to spook him."

Jack nodded, letting her lead as they followed Dimitri down a twisting staircase into the hotel's underground parking garage. The shadows stretched, long and deep, broken only by the muted glow of security lights.

Dimitri approached a sleek black sedan parked in the far corner, his pace quick, his stance alert. Jack held up a hand, signaling Irina to stop as he pulled out his phone, watching the tracking beacon light up on his screen.

"He's headed downtown," Jack murmured. "Ready for a tail?"

Irina nodded, already moving toward the silver sedan she'd arranged. "Try to keep it subtle."

Jack slid into the passenger seat, casting her a sidelong look. "Subtle is my specialty."

She rolled her eyes, turning the ignition. "Just buckle up, Jones."

They waited as Dimitri's car pulled out, keeping a safe distance as he threaded his way through New York's streets toward the East River. After crossing the bridge into Brooklyn, the city lights faded, replaced by an industrial sprawl as they neared the waterfront.

Farrow's voice crackled over the comm in Jack's ear. "Where's he headed?"

"Brooklyn docks," Jack replied as Dimitri turned into a deserted warehouse district. "Not exactly a runway."

"Stay sharp," Farrow warned. "You're on your own, and we have limited intel on Isaac's activity in the area."

Dimitri parked near a chain-link fence surrounding a row of warehouses. Irina cut their headlights and pulled to a stop at a safe distance.

"Looks like a drop," she whispered, her eyes tracking Dimitri as he stepped out of the car, a slim briefcase clutched under his arm.

Jack shifted. "He's not here for small talk."

Irina's gaze hardened. "We move—quietly."

They slipped from the car and moved through the shadows, staying hidden behind shipping containers. Jack strained his ears but caught only the distant lapping of water against the pier.

Dimitri approached a dimly lit doorway, knocking twice. The door opened, revealing the silhouette of a tall man in a trench coat. Dimitri handed over the briefcase, saying something too low to hear.

Jack's pulse quickened. "It's a handoff. We need to know what's in that case."

Irina's hand tightened on his arm. "Not yet. If we move now, we risk everything."

But Jack had already started forward, his focus locked on the exchange. He crept closer, crouching behind a stack of wooden pallets, now only a few feet from where Dimitri and the stranger stood.

The man in the trench coat opened the briefcase, flipping through what looked like documents—maps and photographs. Jack squinted, straining to make out the details.

Just then, the man looked up, his gaze sweeping the area. Jack froze as the man's eyes hovered over his hiding spot for a second too long.

"Seems we have company, Mr. Fedorov," the man said, his voice low and thickly accented.

Dimitri's eyes widened, but before he could react, the man seized him by the shoulder, pulling him into the shadows. Jack cursed under his breath, preparing to act, but Irina's hand gripped his arm, keeping him still.

"Wait," she hissed, her gaze flashing with urgency. "If we rush in, we lose everything."

Jack's jaw clenched, instincts warring with logic, but he stayed put, watching as Dimitri and his contact vanished deeper into the warehouse.

Irina's grip lingered, her voice a whisper. "Remember, Jack—Isaac's people don't hesitate to kill."

Jack's tension broke through, his voice rougher than intended. "And what's stopping you, Irina? I've seen agents turn before. One wrong move, and you'd sell me out without a second thought."

Her eyes narrowed, her whisper icy. "Careful, Jones. Your theatrics aren't helping. I'm here because my orders align with yours. If you're too paranoid to see that, it's your problem. But stay sharp—anything less and you're dead."

Jack studied her, his gaze piercing as he searched for any tell, any flicker of betrayal. NESA had hung him out to dry more than once, sending him on missions where he was practically cut loose. The idea of EISA pulling the same trick was all too real.

He forced himself to look away, tension coiled in his muscles. "Fine. Stay sharp, stay focused. But know this—if you veer, NESA will be watching."

Irina's tone remained composed. "Understood. But trust me, this mission doesn't hinge on us trusting each other. It hinges on taking down Isaac's operation without a hint of compromise."

They moved in sync, slipping into the warehouse after Dimitri and his contact. Inside, the warehouse was dark, the air thick with dust and the smell of rusted metal. Jack's gaze darted through the shadows until he caught sight of Dimitri's blond hair, following his contact toward the far end of the building.

Irina gestured toward a metal staircase leading to a second-floor catwalk. "We'll get a better view from up there."

They ascended carefully, each step calculated to avoid detection. From the catwalk, Jack saw Dimitri and the man in the trench coat standing beneath a flickering light.

Dimitri was speaking quickly, his voice tense. "Isaac promised protection—he assured me."

The man chuckled, his tone laced with menace. "Protection isn't cheap, Fedorov. Your role is clear—deliver, and Isaac rewards. But don't mistake value for invincibility."

Dimitri swallowed, glancing around nervously. "If they find out—"

"They won't," the man interrupted, voice cold. "Remember, you're useful—but not irreplaceable."

Jack's stomach twisted. Dimitri was trapped, a pawn in Isaac's operation with no way out. Irina leaned closer, her whisper barely audible. "You hear that?"

"Yeah," Jack replied, grim. "Isaac's got him bound tight. One wrong move, and Dimitri's expendable."

As they watched, the man in the trench coat handed Dimitri a new briefcase, something metallic glinting inside—a gun, fully assembled.

Dimitri's face blanched as the man's instructions cut through the silence. "Your next target is at the Embassy Gala tomorrow night. Make it clear who sent you."

Dimitri nodded reluctantly, tucking the briefcase under his arm. Jack's chest tightened—Dimitri was about to be used as a weapon in Isaac's game.

Jack turned to Irina, urgency flashing in his gaze. "We have to intervene."

Irina nodded but held up a hand. "Not now. We pull him out now, and Isaac goes underground. We can't afford to lose this lead."

Reluctantly, Jack nodded, the weight of the decision settling heavily. He kept his voice steady, but firm. "Fine. But when we have the chance, I'm pulling him out—intel or no intel."

Irina gave him a curt nod. "Agreed. But we're here to dismantle the syndicate, not jeopardize everything for one operative."

As they slipped out of the warehouse and into the night, Jack knew the line between allies and operatives had never been thinner.

CHAPTER 4
BETRAYAL IN THE SHADOWS

JACK PACED the cramped hotel room he and Irina had rented in Brooklyn, his gaze flicking to the closed door. Outside, the streets of the industrial district were quiet, shadowed under low, storm-heavy clouds. He glanced back to see Irina seated at the small table by the window, her expression unreadable as she scanned intel reports on her tablet.

Finally, he broke the silence. "So, we're just supposed to wait here while Dimitri gears up for his next target?"

Irina's fingers hovered over the screen, but her face remained impassive. "We can't move until we know who he's targeting and how. Jumping too soon risks losing every connection to Isaac's network."

Jack exhaled sharply, forcing down his frustration. "And if that means someone dies at this 'Embassy Gala'? Can you really stomach that?"

She looked up, her green eyes cold. "This isn't about feelings, Jack. It's about the mission. One mistake, and Isaac vanishes, taking every lead with him. We need patience."

"Patience?" Jack's voice dropped to a hard edge. "You're prepared to let innocent people die just to chase Isaac's shadow?"

Her jaw tightened. "It's not ideal, but if saving one life tonight means losing the chance to end Isaac's operation, then yes, patience.

This syndicate kills on a scale far beyond what one body count can measure. Sometimes, sacrifices are necessary."

"Maybe that's how you operate," Jack muttered, his voice low with bitterness. "But I don't leave people behind. Not if I can help it."

Irina's gaze softened slightly, but her tone stayed firm. "Don't think I haven't faced those choices, Jack. I know what it's like to lose people and make the hard calls. If you want to catch Isaac, then accept that sometimes, the mission has to come first."

Jack studied her face, searching for any crack in her icy resolve, but her expression was guarded. He took a breath, letting the tension settle between them. "Fine. But we act the moment Dimitri makes contact with his target."

Irina nodded, her focus shifting back to her tablet. But Jack noticed the faint tension in her posture, the flicker of something like doubt in her eyes. Perhaps he wasn't the only one divided between the mission and the morality of it.

The next hour passed in a tense silence, both of them waiting for word from the field team trailing Dimitri. Jack turned his attention to the Embassy Gala invitation they'd acquired—an embossed card meant for Manhattan's elite. The guest list included high-ranking diplomats, politicians, and executives from across the globe.

His frown deepened as he considered the stakes. "If Isaac's ordered a hit, this isn't just a body count—it could be an international disaster."

Irina glanced up, her expression contemplative. "Which is exactly what Isaac wants. Chaos gives him room to operate unnoticed."

A notification beeped on her tablet, and she leaned forward, reading intently. "Dimitri's on the move. He's headed to a safe house near Midtown."

Jack straightened, adrenaline sharpening his focus. "Then it's time."

An hour later, they were in Midtown, watching from a narrow alley as Dimitri exited his black sedan and slipped into a nondescript building. The location was a stark contrast to last night's industrial sprawl—clean, low-profile, tucked amid the bustling heart of the city. Jack noted Dimitri's unhurried pace, his professional precision.

Irina signaled for Jack to follow as they approached the building's side entrance. Using the credentials Farrow had supplied, they unlocked a secure door, moving with the stealth of seasoned operatives. The dimly lit interior smelled of old carpet and disinfectant, every footstep absorbed by thick carpeting.

They climbed a narrow stairway, the voices at the end of the hallway growing louder with each step. Jack strained to hear, catching fragments as he and Irina crouched by the door.

"...at the gala tonight. No mistakes, understood?" The voice was clipped, with a thick Russian accent.

Dimitri replied, his tone uncertain. "I... I understand. But security is tight. I'll need a diversion to get close to him."

Jack and Irina exchanged a look. Whoever Dimitri was talking to had issued direct orders. If they played this right, they could learn the target's identity and possibly leverage Dimitri.

Irina leaned close, her whisper barely audible. "I'll create a distraction. Slip inside and get what you can."

Jack smirked. "Think you can handle a distraction?"

Her look was almost amused. "Just don't get caught."

With a nod, she stood and strode down the hallway, her steps soft. Jack listened as she knocked on a nearby door, her accent thick as she called out, "Excuse me? I think I'm lost. Can someone help me?"

Inside, the voices stilled, followed by footsteps approaching the door. As it opened, Jack flattened himself against the wall, holding his breath while a man stepped into the hall, drawn by Irina's feigned distress.

Seizing his chance, Jack slipped into the room, crouching behind a stack of crates as he took in the small, dim space. A map lay spread on a table in the center, red circles marking the Embassy and surrounding streets. Jack edged closer, snapping photos of the map with his phone.

A voice cut through the silence. "You think you can sneak in here without me noticing?"

Jack straightened, facing Dimitri, who stood by the window, a mix of fear and defiance in his expression.

"Not sneaking," Jack replied, slipping his phone back into his pocket. "Just checking in on an old friend."

Dimitri's jaw tightened. "I don't have friends. Not anymore."

Jack raised a hand, keeping his tone calm. "Listen, Dimitri. You're in over your head. Whatever Isaac promised, it's not worth your life. We can protect you if you work with us."

Dimitri scoffed, crossing his arms. "Protection? From Isaac? You have no idea. He's everywhere. One wrong move, and I'm dead."

Jack took a step forward, his gaze unyielding. "Then you're already dead if you don't cooperate. Isaac won't leave you alive if you fail tonight. This is your chance to start over. We can help you disappear."

For a moment, Dimitri's face softened, a flicker of hope in his eyes, quickly masked by defiance. "Why should I trust you? For all I know, you're here to kill me."

"If that were the plan," Jack replied dryly, "we wouldn't be talking."

Dimitri searched Jack's face, looking for any sign of deception. After a tense silence, he exhaled shakily, glancing at the door as if expecting someone to burst in.

Irina stepped back into the room, her expression unreadable as she took in the scene. She looked at Jack, her gaze questioning.

"He's listening," Jack confirmed.

Irina turned her attention to Dimitri, her tone precise. "You have two options, Dimitri. Follow through with Isaac's plan and hope he doesn't discard you afterward, or work with us. Who's the target tonight?"

Dimitri gripped the edge of the table, his knuckles white. He looked between them, fear shadowing his face.

Finally, he whispered, "The French ambassador. He's... Isaac's target."

Jack exchanged a glance with Irina, his mind racing. An embassy assassination targeting a high-ranking diplomat—a precise, calculated hit engineered for maximum chaos.

Irina nodded, her expression hardening. "Then we don't have time to waste. We'll get you out of here, but you'll follow our lead."

Dimitri's voice trembled. "If Isaac finds out I talked—"

"He won't," Jack assured him. "We'll move you to a safe house before he has a chance. But you have to trust us."

Dimitri nodded, his fear-laced decision clear. "All right. I'll do as you say."

Jack placed a steadying hand on his shoulder. "Good choice. Now let's get moving."

As they headed for the door, Jack caught Irina's eye. She was as unreadable as ever, her gaze forward and determined. Yet he sensed that this mission was now far more dangerous than either of them had expected. Together, they would have to navigate Isaac's deadly game, knowing that any misstep could be their last.

And as they led Dimitri into the night, Jack's resolve solidified. He didn't fully trust Irina, but he knew one thing—no matter what it took, he'd see this mission through.

CHAPTER 5
THE GALA GAMBIT

THE EMBASSY GALA was in full swing by the time Jack, Irina, and Dimitri arrived. The grand hall shimmered with diplomats, high-ranking officials, and guests in black-tie elegance, illuminated by chandeliers casting a warm glow. Beneath the sophistication, a current of tension thrummed through the air, thinly veiling the night's peril. Near the stage, the French and American ambassadors mingled, unaware that Isaac's plot was unfolding around them.

Jack's gaze swept the room, noting potential exits, vantage points, and every shadowed corner. He felt Dimitri's anxiety beside him, the young man's hands gripping a cocktail glass like a lifeline. Irina moved gracefully at Jack's side, her expression calm, though her eyes were as vigilant as his. The plan was simple: keep Dimitri close, then slip him out before Isaac's men noticed.

"Stay focused," Jack murmured. "No sudden moves."

Dimitri nodded, his gaze darting around. "He's watching, isn't he? Isaac has people here?"

"Maybe," Jack replied, keeping his tone calm. "But you stick with us, and you're safe."

Irina flashed Dimitri a reassuring smile, though a flicker of tension showed in her eyes. "Remember what we discussed—follow our lead, and you're out of this by morning."

As they moved through the crowd, Jack sensed a shift in the atmosphere—a few faces watching them a beat too long, expressions held carefully neutral. Isaac's men were here, tracking Dimitri, waiting for him to make his move.

Jack leaned close to Irina, his voice low. "Isaac's people are here. They're watching Dimitri."

Her jaw tightened as she surveyed the room. "Then we need to act fast. The French ambassador's about to speak. If Dimitri doesn't follow through, they'll notice."

Jack's mind raced, calculating their next steps. "We get him out quietly. If it looks like he did the job, Isaac's men won't follow."

Irina's gaze locked on Dimitri. "Can you fake it?"

Dimitri's eyes widened. "Fake it? You mean… pretend?"

Jack gripped his shoulder, steadying him. "Isaac has eyes everywhere. But if we make it look like you finished the job, we can slip out before they know what's happened."

Dimitri's face paled. "I… I'll try. But what if they catch on?"

"We improvise," Irina said firmly. "Stick with Jack. I'll cover us."

She wove her way through the crowd toward the main exit, positioning herself where she could intercept any sudden moves. Jack guided Dimitri to the back of the room, where a table covered in glassware and linens offered some cover.

"Take out the gun," Jack whispered, his tone calm. "Just don't aim it at anyone. We'll create a distraction—make it look like you're taking the shot."

Hands shaking, Dimitri pulled the pistol from his jacket, his face pale under the chandelier lights. Jack gave him a quick nod of reassurance.

"You're doing fine," Jack said. "Hold it up for a few seconds, then lower it."

Dimitri nodded, lifting the gun, his movements stiff and unnatural. Jack caught Irina's eye across the room; she gave a small nod, signaling she was ready.

In an instant, the tension snapped.

Irina "accidentally" toppled a champagne tower, sending glass and bubbles crashing across the floor. Guests gasped, turning toward the noise, and Jack seized the moment.

"Now," he whispered to Dimitri.

Dimitri lifted the gun just slightly, pointing it vaguely toward the ambassador before lowering it. The quick flash of movement was enough to satisfy Isaac's men, who relaxed slightly as they caught sight of him lowering the weapon, thinking the job done.

Jack signaled to Irina, who was already moving toward them, eyes locked on the exit. "Let's go."

They moved swiftly through the dim corridors leading out of the embassy, their footsteps quick and quiet. Jack's senses were on high alert, pulse thudding as he steered Dimitri through the maze of hallways. His priority: a clean escape. Questions would come later.

The frosty night air hit them as they stepped outside, and Jack scanned the empty street for threats. Irina led them to a car parked in the shadows, and they climbed in, tension easing slightly as they sped away from the embassy.

"Did it work?" Dimitri's voice was a shaky whisper.

Irina nodded, her gaze sharp. "For now. But we'll get you to a safe house before Isaac's men realize you're gone."

As they drove away from Manhattan's gleaming lights, Jack felt his adrenaline fading, replaced by a grim resolve. They'd slipped Dimitri out, but Isaac's retaliation would be swift and brutal.

The safe house was a modest apartment in Queens, far from the luxury of the embassy gala. Inside, they secured the doors and checked the windows before letting Dimitri settle onto a worn sofa. Jack watched him, noting the tremor in his hands, the haunted look in his eyes. Dimitri was in way over his head.

Irina stood by the window, peering through the blinds. "We're clear. For now."

Jack turned to Dimitri, his tone serious. "You did well tonight. But this is just the start. Isaac's won't let this go. We need everything you know about his network if we're going to keep you safe."

Dimitri's gaze was distant, haunted. "I'll tell you what I can. But Isaac... he has people everywhere. You have no idea how powerful he is."

Jack's jaw tightened. "We know. That's why we need to move fast. Once he realizes you're missing, he'll send his best to hunt you down."

Irina crossed the room, her expression steely. "Start from the beginning. What's Isaac's network look like? Every safe house, contact, and hideout. If we're going to protect you, we need the whole picture."

Dimitri hesitated, glancing between them as if weighing his options. Finally, he nodded, resignation heavy on his shoulders.

"All right," he said, voice barely above a whisper. "I'll tell you. But once he finds out I've betrayed him, he won't stop coming after me. Or you."

Jack met his gaze, his voice unwavering. "We can handle it. Start talking."

Dimitri took a breath, gaze fixed on his hands as he began. "Isaac has a network across Europe and Asia—safe houses, contacts, insiders in Interpol and customs. He only stays at each location for a few days, moving constantly to avoid detection."

Irina's eyes narrowed. "And tonight's gala—was there more to it?"

Dimitri's face darkened. "Tonight was a message. Isaac thrives on chaos. An assassination at the embassy would've shattered alliances, created instability. Fear is his currency—it keeps him untouchable."

Jack felt a chill. This wasn't just organized crime; it was calculated destabilization, designed to ripple across nations.

Irina's expression hardened, a cold resolve in her gaze. "Then we need more than just your intel, Dimitri. We need proof. Records, documents—something concrete that ties Isaac to his operation."

Dimitri shook his head, dread darkening his features. "Isaac keeps his files in one place. A base in Siberia, deep in the mountains. It's a fortress. Even I've never been there."

Jack and Irina exchanged a glance, silent understanding passing between them. Siberia—if Isaac kept his secrets there, that's where they'd go.

Irina spoke with quiet determination. "Then that's our next move. We'll find his base, get the proof, and dismantle his operation once and for all."

Dimitri's face paled. "You'll never get out alive. His guards—

mercenaries, ex-military—they'll kill you before you even set foot on the property."

Jack's mouth twisted into a grim smile. "We'll take our chances."

But as the weight of their mission settled over them, he couldn't ignore the nagging feeling that they were stepping into a trap. Isaac had always been a step ahead, and now they were following his trail into the lion's den.

Irina met his gaze, her eyes reflecting the same determination—and the same unease. They were both in too deep to turn back now.

"Then we go to Siberia," she said, her voice steady. "And we finish this."

Jack nodded, a pulse of anticipation and fear thrumming through him. Isaac had drawn the battle lines, and now it was their turn to strike. But as he looked at Irina, he couldn't shake the feeling that the actual battle wasn't just against Isaac—it was against the trust he didn't dare give her.

One way or another, their alliance was about to face its greatest test.

CHAPTER 6
INTO THE LION'S DEN

THE WIND HOWLED as Jack stared out over the Siberian landscape, an endless expanse of ice and jagged mountains stretching beneath the helicopter. The rotors sliced through the air, vibrating under each gust that battered the aircraft. Across from him, Irina sat, her face as unyielding as the terrain below. Dimitri, looking pale, huddled between them, his gaze darting anxiously as the chopper descended.

The pilot's voice crackled through Jack's headset. "This is as close as I can get you. Isaac's compound is ten miles north—you'll need to go on foot from here."

Jack nodded, gripping his seat as the helicopter dipped lower, hovering just above the snow-covered ground. As the door slid open, an icy wind slammed into him, and he took a deep breath, steeling himself.

"Let's move," he called, signaling to Irina and Dimitri.

One by one, they leapt into the snow, their boots crunching into the thick, frozen ground. The helicopter kicked up a blinding flurry before it veered away, disappearing into a sky thick with stormy clouds.

Irina pulled out a GPS device, her fingers deft despite the biting cold. "Isaac's compound is through the valley. We'll need a direct route if we want to reach it by nightfall."

Jack looked at Dimitri, whose face was taut with fear, though he nodded firmly. "I didn't come this far to turn back."

Jack turned to Irina. "Lead the way."

They trudged forward, each step laborious in the thick snow, silence broken only by the whistle of the wind and the crunch of their boots. Jack scanned their surroundings, alert for movement; Isaac's compound was a fortress, guarded by operatives who'd be expecting trouble.

As they climbed over a ridge, the wind eased. Irina checked the GPS, pointing to a narrow path between two cliffs. "We'll be visible in the pass, but it's the only way through."

Jack nodded, hand instinctively moving to the pistol at his side. "Then we keep it quick."

They pressed on, hugging the shadowed rock walls as they descended into the pass. The deeper they went, the colder the air grew, shadows closing in around them. Jack's pulse quickened, his senses sharp with anticipation. They were close now; he could feel the weight of Isaac's presence looming over the valley.

Dimitri stumbled, his breath harsh in the cold air, and Irina reached out, steadying him with a firm grip. Jack watched them, suspicion tightening in his gut. Was she protecting him—or keeping something hidden?

They rounded a bend, and the compound came into view: a sprawling, fortified stronghold nestled between cliffs, its walls reinforced with concrete and razor wire, guard towers positioned at each corner.

Irina dropped to a crouch behind a rock, pulling Jack and Dimitri down with her. She pointed to a narrow gap between two towers, where a lone guard patrolled. "That's our entry point. There's a blind spot in the guard rotation—ninety seconds to get through before the next patrol."

Jack's gaze focused on the guard. "We'll need a distraction."

Irina reached into her pack, pulling out a small explosive. "Thirty feet east. When it detonates, we go."

Jack raised an eyebrow. "Efficient."

A faint smile flickered across her face. "It's what I do."

They waited as she crept forward, placing the explosive out of sight before returning to their cover. She set the timer, and seconds later, a muffled blast echoed through the valley, followed by the shouts of guards and the blare of alarms.

"Now," Irina whispered, leading them toward the gap in the wall.

They moved swiftly, staying low as they slipped into the compound. Inside, dim lights and shadows cast an eerie stillness over the maze of corridors and stairwells. Jack tightened his grip on his pistol, following Irina as she led them deeper into Isaac's stronghold. Pausing at a metal door, she quickly set up a keypad override, the tension palpable as they waited. With a soft beep, the lock disengaged.

Inside, rows of shelves held crates and files, papers spilling over the edges. Dimitri's eyes widened. "This... this is everything. His entire operation."

Jack scanned the room, mind racing. "If we get evidence of Isaac's network, it could dismantle everything."

Irina moved to a crate, pulling out a stack of files. She leafed through them, her eyes narrowing as she skimmed the contents. "Assassination orders, smuggling routes—it's all here."

They worked quickly, gathering as many documents as they could carry. Dimitri's hands shook as he flipped through the files, fear and determination battling on his face.

Jack kept an ear on the hallway outside, glancing at Irina as she moved between crates. She paused, her expression shifting for a split second as she examined a particular file.

"What is it?" Jack murmured, stepping closer.

She looked up; her face neutral. "Just... the scope of his reach. It's worse than I thought."

He eyed her for a moment, but let it go. They were in the heart of Isaac's compound, and distractions could be fatal.

Just as they finished gathering the files, footsteps echoed down the corridor. Jack's hand tightened around his pistol as he signaled for silence.

The footsteps grew louder, stopping just outside the door. Jack held his breath, weapon ready. Then the footsteps receded, fading into the distance.

He exhaled slowly, glancing at Irina and Dimitri. "We need to move. Now."

They slipped into the corridor, dashing through the dimly lit maze. But as they turned a corner, a guard stepped into their path, gun raised.

"Freeze!" the guard shouted.

Jack moved on instinct, closing the distance in a heartbeat. With a swift twist, he disarmed the guard, knocking him out cold as his body crumpled to the floor.

Irina gave him a curt nod, her voice low. "Nice reflexes."

"Keep moving," he replied, leading them down the hallway.

They reached the exit without further incident, slipping through the gap in the wall and back into the icy cliffs. As they navigated the pass, Jack's sense of being watched returned.

Irina seemed to feel it too, her gaze sharp as she looked over her shoulder. When they reached the top of the ridge, she stopped, her face tense.

"We're not alone."

Jack scanned the valley below, spotting figures moving toward them from the compound—Isaac's men, heavily armed and closing in fast.

"Run," he said, his voice urgent.

They broke into a sprint, boots pounding against the snow as they raced for the extraction point. The wind whipped around them, stinging their faces, but they didn't slow. The sound of pursuit grew louder, closer.

Dimitri stumbled, his breath labored, and Jack grabbed his arm, pulling him forward. "Keep going! We're almost there!"

They crested the ridge, the extraction point in sight. Above, the steady thrum of helicopter blades broke through the wind. Relief surged as the chopper appeared, hovering just above the ground.

"Get in!" Jack shouted, pushing Dimitri toward the open door.

Irina climbed in after him, her expression steely as she helped Dimitri into his seat. Jack was the last to board, gripping the door as the helicopter lifted into the sky.

Below, Isaac's men gathered at the cliff's edge, their faces masks of frustration as their prey escaped. Jack couldn't resist a slight smile, a sense of triumph surging through him.

But a glance at Irina showed tension lingering in her eyes, shadows of doubt that hadn't faded. They'd escaped, but Isaac wouldn't stop— not until one side was dead.

As the helicopter sped away from the compound, Jack knew one thing for certain: their mission had only just begun.

CHAPTER 7
CRACKS IN THE ICE

THE SAFE HOUSE sat isolated in the Russian wilderness, a rugged cabin encircled by dense pine forests. Jack stood at the window, watching the snow drift down, his body still tense from their escape. Even with the cabin's relative safety, his instincts stayed sharp—Isaac's reach was vast, and he couldn't let his guard down.

Across the room, Irina and Dimitri sat at a small wooden table, sifting through the files taken from Isaac's compound. Maps, photos, coded messages, and encrypted documents sprawled across the table in a chaotic mess. Dimitri's face was pale, his hands shaking slightly as he examined one of the papers.

Jack's gaze shifted to him. "Take a breath, Dimitri. We're safe for now."

Dimitri nodded, though a haunted look remained in his eyes. "I never thought it would come to this. Isaac has people everywhere. People I thought were friends, colleagues. It's like he's always a step ahead."

Irina's eyes flicked up to meet Jack's. "That's because he is. And if we're going to stop him, we need to move fast. We have enough intel here to map out his network, but we'll need help decoding it."

Jack's brow lifted, his tone skeptical. "Help? And who exactly do we trust with that? Isaac has his hooks in every agency."

Irina's jaw tightened. "Not everyone. I've kept contact with a few within EISA and NESA—people I know we can rely on."

Jack's eyes narrowed, suspicion prickling at him. "When exactly were you planning to mention these contacts?"

She met his gaze, her voice steady. "My orders were explicit: operate independently and report to select contacts. NESA signed off on it."

Jack's tone hardened. "And what about your loyalty, Irina? Keeping things hidden could compromise this mission. Who's really pulling the strings here?"

Irina's eyes flashed, sharp and resolute. "You're questioning my loyalty? After everything we've been through?"

Dimitri glanced between them, clearly uncomfortable but saying nothing. The air thickened with tension.

"I'm questioning your secrets," Jack replied. "Trust goes both ways. Right now, I'm in the dark."

Irina's expression softened, though her gaze remained guarded. "I'm not your enemy, Jack. I want Isaac finished as much as you do. But we're up against forces larger than either of us, and trusting the wrong person could be fatal."

Jack held her gaze, unwilling to let the matter drop. Before he could press further, Dimitri cleared his throat.

"I... I think I've found something," Dimitri said, holding up a sheet of paper with a series of numbers and letters scrawled across it.

Jack glanced over, studying the code. "A coordinates cipher. If we can crack this, we'll have locations for Isaac's remaining safe houses."

Irina leaned in, her eyes narrowing as she examined the numbers. "We'll need a decryption key. It's probably buried somewhere in these files."

Dimitri's face brightened with a glimmer of hope. "I might be able to help. Isaac's code expert was obsessed with patterns. If we can spot the key sequence, I should be able to decode it."

Jack nodded, setting aside his suspicion for now. "Let's get to it."

They worked in silence for the next hour, searching the files for anything that matched the cipher. Jack's fingers grew numb in the cold, but he ignored it, focused on unraveling the threads of Isaac's network.

Names, locations, connections—it all painted a vivid picture of Isaac's reach.

Finally, Irina held up a document with a series of dates and numbers. "This matches the cipher pattern. Dates and locations for arms shipments."

Dimitri's face lit up. "Yes, that's it. I can decode the coordinates with this."

As Dimitri set to work, Jack's mind drifted back to Irina. Despite her skill in the field, her secrets gnawed at him, forming an invisible wall between them.

After a few minutes, Dimitri exhaled in relief. "Got it! These coordinates lead to a location in southern Russia—one of Isaac's larger safe houses."

Jack frowned at the decoded location. "What would he store there?"

Dimitri's face darkened. "Information. Records, transaction logs, even the identities of his network members. It's like his personal archive."

Irina's gaze sharpened. "If we get that, we could dismantle his entire operation."

Jack nodded, feeling a surge of determination. "Then that's our target. We'll hit the safe house and retrieve the archive. But we'll need to be careful—Isaac won't make this easy."

Dimitri swallowed, dread filling his eyes. "If he finds out we're going after his records, he'll kill us."

Jack's hand landed firmly on Dimitri's shoulder. "We knew the risks coming in. We're not turning back now."

Irina began gathering the documents, slipping them into her pack. "Agreed. We move at dawn. The sooner we hit that safe house, the better."

The rest of the night passed in tense preparation, each of them checking weapons, reviewing maps, and rehearsing scenarios. Outside, the snow had stopped, leaving a silent world blanketed in white, as though the wilderness itself awaited the storm they were about to unleash.

As dawn approached, Jack found himself alone with Irina in the cabin's small kitchen. She was focused, cleaning her gun, tension radiating from her. Breaking the silence, he cleared his throat.

"About earlier," he began quietly. "I get that you have orders. But if there's anything I should know—anything that could affect this mission—now's the time."

Irina's gaze met his, her expression unreadable. "You want the truth?"

He nodded. "I need it."

She hesitated, her voice softening for a moment. "Isaac and I have history. Years ago, I was part of an undercover operation in his network. I got close to him. But when my cover was blown, he turned on me. He's been after me ever since."

Jack's jaw tightened, processing her words. "And you didn't think to mention this sooner?"

She met his gaze, her tone steady. "I'm following protocol. I was under orders to act independently, not disclose everything to NESA. Operational security is critical."

Jack's expression remained tense, the suspicion in his voice unmistakable. "EISA's protocol or not, keeping secrets doesn't exactly inspire confidence, Irina. I need to know where your loyalties lie."

Irina's eyes narrowed, her tone matching his intensity. "I'm here to stop Isaac, same as you. But some things are on a need-to-know basis. If you can't trust that, then maybe this mission is more complicated than you realize."

Dimitri, glancing between them, broke the silence with a nervous cough. "Whatever this is, can we table it? Isaac's men could be closing in."

Jack cast a final hard look at Irina. "Fine. But after this, we're going to have a serious talk about agency transparency." He softened slightly. "For now, we focus."

Irina's jaw tightened, but she nodded. "Agreed. Let's stay on task."

The dawn light crept over the horizon, casting a faint glow over the cabin. Dimitri joined them, his expression resolute despite his nerves. They gathered their gear, each steeling themselves for what lay ahead.

As they prepared to leave, Jack shot a last glance at Irina, noting her rigid stance and expressionless gaze. Her focus was unwavering, but he couldn't shake the feeling that her resolve might hide something more. Irina's loyalty was as difficult to read as the landscape around them, veiled in secrets and cold resolve. He thought of the operatives he'd known who'd been left to fend for themselves by higher-ups who played them as pawns—agents like Riley, left stranded in Moscow, considered "expendable."

Gripping his weapon, Jack felt the weight of that distrust. Irina's fierce commitment could be professional dedication—or manipulation. His loyalty would stay where it belonged: with NESA and his own survival. He'd proceed cautiously, trusting only himself.

They stepped into the chilly morning, the biting air a harsh welcome as they began their journey toward Isaac's stronghold. Whatever lay ahead, Jack was ready to face it. Whether or not he could trust Irina remained uncertain, but he would see this mission through to the end.

As they trudged forward, their figures growing smaller against the vast wilderness, Jack steeled himself. This wasn't just a battle against Isaac; it was a test of the thin, fraying trust between him and Irina. And he wasn't prepared to gamble with his life—or the mission—for anything less than absolute certainty.

CHAPTER 8
BREAKING THE WEB

THE SUN WAS BARELY a hint on the horizon as Jack, Irina, and Dimitri crept through the dense underbrush surrounding Isaac's southern Russia compound. Trees loomed overhead, their branches heavy with icicles that glittered faintly in the morning light. They moved in silence, their breath fogging in the icy air, their footsteps softened by the packed snow.

Jack scanned the surroundings, noting every shadow and sound that could signal danger. Isaac's men were notorious for their vigilance, and Jack knew they'd defend the stronghold with lethal force. He glanced back at Dimitri, who struggled to keep up, his face pale but resolute. Irina led them with steady focus, checking the GPS as they approached their target. The mission was straightforward in theory: break in, retrieve Isaac's personal archive, and extract as quickly as possible.

They reached a ridge overlooking the compound, shielded by a row of pines. Jack crouched beside Irina, raising his binoculars to study the fortress below. Isaac's stronghold was massive—fortified walls, razor-wire fencing, guard towers at each corner, and rows of armed men patrolling the perimeter.

Dimitri crouched beside them, breathing hard. "How are we supposed to get in? It looks… impossible."

Irina didn't blink as she surveyed the compound. "Not impossible. Just difficult."

Jack lowered his binoculars. "We'll need a weak spot in their defenses. Somewhere we can slip through without triggering alarms."

Irina nodded, her tone calm but firm. "The main entrance is too risky. There's an old drainage tunnel on the western side—if we access it, we might get in undetected."

Dimitri's face was tight with fear. "And if they see us?"

"Then we improvise," Jack said flatly. "You wanted to bring Isaac down. Now's your chance to help make it happen."

Dimitri swallowed but nodded, a flicker of determination crossing his face. Jack turned to Irina. "Lead the way."

They moved swiftly, crouching low as they descended the ridge and approached the western side of the compound. Jack's pulse quickened as they neared the drainage tunnel, half-buried in snow and shadowed by trees. It was narrow, barely wide enough for one person, and smelled faintly of damp earth and rust.

Irina knelt beside the entrance, studying it before glancing at Jack. "This should lead to the lower levels. Once inside, we'll need to move fast."

Jack nodded, hand on his pistol as he motioned for Dimitri to follow. "Stay close. No sound," he ordered.

They slipped into the tunnel; the darkness closing around them as they moved through the cramped space. Every sound echoed; Jack's senses stayed razor sharp, his pulse steady.

When they emerged in a dim corridor, Jack held up a hand, signaling silence. A faint hum pulsed through the walls, the compound feeling alive with a hidden threat.

Irina's whisper was barely audible. "This way."

They crept through the corridors, avoiding the pools of light cast by overhead fixtures. Jack's mind mapped each turn, cataloging exits and escape routes as they moved deeper into the maze-like structure. They'd need every detail committed to memory if they hoped to get out.

At last, they reached a door marked Архивы ("Archives"). Irina inspected the keypad and quickly punched in a series of numbers. The light blinked green, and the door clicked open.

Inside, shelves lined the walls, each one filled with metal filing cabinets. Maps and charts covered the walls. Jack's gaze swept over the documents, and he felt an icy knot in his stomach. Isaac's operation spanned continents, infiltrating governments, corporations, intelligence agencies—a sprawling web of corruption and control.

Dimitri's face was ghostly as he took in the files. "He has... connections everywhere. This is so much worse than I thought."

Irina moved to the cabinet, pulling out a thick file and flipping through it. "It's all here. Names, locations, financial records. With this, we can dismantle everything."

Jack grabbed a file marked Operations, his eyes scanning the pages. "These are assassination orders. High-ranking politicians, CEOs, military officials. Isaac's been orchestrating hits across Europe."

He turned to Irina, his expression grim. "This intel could destroy his entire network if we get it to NESA and EISA."

Irina nodded, her eyes sharp. "But we need to be careful. Isaac's reach extends everywhere—his people will come after us the moment they realize what we've taken."

They stuffed packing files into their bags. Then a faint beeping echoed through the room, and Jack froze. The sound was unmistakable —the alarm had been triggered.

"Move!" he hissed, slinging his bag over his shoulder and sprinting for the door.

They burst into the hallway as the alarm blared, echoing through the compound. Jack's pulse pounded as he scanned their surroundings. Footsteps thundered closer, and he drew his pistol, motioning for Irina and Dimitri to follow.

They darted through the corridors, the thundering footsteps and shouts of guards hot on their trail. Jack calculated every turn, every route, hunting for an exit.

As they rounded a corner, a squad of guards appeared in their path. Jack fired instinctively, the crack of gunfire ringing out as the nearest guard went down. Irina fired beside him, her shots swift and precise.

"Go!" Jack barked, pushing Dimitri ahead as they sprinted toward a stairwell.

They climbed fast, their legs burning, each step carrying them closer to the surface. They burst onto the roof, gasping as the frosty night air struck them. Below, the compound was in chaos, guards swarming as lights flashed across the grounds. A helicopter hovered nearby, its spotlight sweeping the area. Relief surged through Jack as he recognized their extraction.

"Signal them!" he called to Irina.

She pulled out a flare, firing it into the sky. The helicopter banked toward them, lowering a rope ladder. Jack motioned Dimitri to go first, steadying him as he grabbed the rungs and started climbing.

"Go," Jack urged Irina.

She hesitated, her gaze meeting his, and he caught a flicker of something unreadable in her expression. Then she nodded, grabbing the ladder and ascending quickly.

Jack was the last up, gripping the rungs as bullets whizzed past. As he scrambled into the helicopter, the door slid shut, and they lifted off, the compound shrinking below them. He leaned back, catching his breath, feeling the weight of their mission settle over him.

They'd done it. The files were in their hands, and with them, the means to dismantle Isaac's empire. But as Jack looked at Irina, he couldn't shake the feeling that their victory came at a cost.

Irina's gaze met his, her face unreadable, a lingering tension between them. They'd fought together, saved each other's lives, yet an invisible barrier remained, an unspoken distrust neither seemed willing to break.

Dimitri's voice broke the silence, filled with awe and relief. "We did it... we actually did it."

Jack forced a smile, clapping Dimitri's shoulder. "It's not over yet. We still have to get this intel back. Isaac's people won't stop coming."

Irina nodded, her expression hardening. "He'll retaliate with everything he has. We need to stay vigilant."

Jack turned to the window, watching the compound fade into the night. The files felt heavy in his bag—the evidence that could topple Isaac's empire.

But as the helicopter flew further from the compound, Jack knew the fight was far from over. Isaac wouldn't go down easily, and neither would his network. They were stepping into a war that would push every limit, challenge every alliance, and force them to confront the secrets that had drawn them together.

Jack glanced at Irina, his jaw set. No matter what lay ahead, he'd see this mission through to the end. But he knew that trust—the trust they could or couldn't place in each other—would be their sharpest weapon or their deadliest risk.

The End

SHADOW PURSUIT

A SHORT THRILLER

CHAPTER 1
INTO THE SYNDICATE'S SHADOWS

JACK JONES ADJUSTED the cufflinks on his borrowed tuxedo, the smooth fabric concealing a holstered pistol. Around him, Zurich's wealthiest elite sipped champagne and murmured among themselves, their laughter low and deliberate—the kind cultivated in shadowy corners, where secrets were currency. He moved through the underground auction like a ghost, detached yet deliberate, every step reminding him of the razor-thin line he walked. He had inhabited scenes like this countless times before, but tonight felt different.

You're doing this for them, he reminded himself, thinking of the small framed photo he always carried in his wallet—his sister's family, all smiles and innocence. If taking down Isaac's network meant sparing them the chaos of another international conflict, it was worth every calculated risk. But the truth gnawed at him: even heroes got their hands dirty in this business, and Jack had long since lost count of the stains on his.

"Jones, status report," Director Farrow's voice crackled in his earpiece.

"Still blending in," Jack replied, his tone casual as he scanned the room. "Not much action yet."

"Keep it that way. We need you sharp when Isaac's buyer shows. If that artifact's as important as we think, it'll lead us straight to his network."

Jack's eyes swept the room, his instincts prickling. The auction's centerpiece, a sleek steel artifact the size of a shoebox, rested beneath a bulletproof glass case on the main stage. The auctioneer had introduced it as a relic of the Cold War, rumored to hold encrypted data tied to long-dormant espionage networks.

It was exactly the kind of thing someone like Isaac would kill for.

Jack's focus shifted as the crowd parted, revealing a familiar figure moving with cat-like grace. His stomach tightened as he recognized the fiery red hair and unmistakable poise.

Irina Stepanov.

She wore a fitted black gown that draped like armor, her green eyes scanning the crowd with the cold precision of a sniper sight. Jack bit back a groan. If she was here, things had just gotten more complicated. He adjusted his position, his gaze fixed on Irina's familiar figure weaving through the crowd. How many times had they stood on opposite sides of the same mission? Her loyalty to EISA was as resolute as his to NESA, yet here they were again, two pawns chasing the same prize in different games.

He clenched his fists, his mind flashing back to Munich—a failed mission that still haunted him. They'd been allies that night, sharing whispered strategies in a freezing safe house, their differences momentarily set aside. But the fallout had been devastating. Lives had been lost, including an informant who had trusted Jack to keep them safe. For the greater good, Farrow had said, but the phrase had long since lost its meaning.

As Jack watched Irina raise her paddle, her movements calm and precise, he wondered how she reconciled the cost of this life. Did she ever feel the weight of it? Or had she learned, as he had, to bury the guilt deep enough that it only surfaced in moments like this—when the stakes demanded it?

"Farrow," Jack muttered into his mic, keeping his tone low. "We've got company. Guess who?"

The line was silent for half a beat before Farrow's voice returned, sharper now. "Stepanov?"

"Who else? EISA's golden girl just waltzed in."

"Keep her in check," Farrow ordered. "If EISA's involved, they're after the artifact too. Don't let her beat you to it."

"Relax, I've got this."

Jack moved to keep Irina in his line of sight, slipping between clusters of patrons. She hadn't seen him yet, but it was only a matter of time. Her paddle rose smoothly during the auction's latest bid, her movements as deliberate as a chess master's opening gambit.

"Twenty million euros," the auctioneer announced, his voice booming across the gilded room.

Irina's bid. Jack frowned. She wasn't just observing—she was in play.

The tension in the room crackled as another paddle rose across the room. The auctioneer seized on it instantly. "Twenty-five million!"

Irina's eyes narrowed, her gaze flicking toward the new bidder. Jack could almost see the gears turning in her head as she recalculated her strategy. For a brief moment, she caught sight of him across the room, her expression hardening into a cool mask.

Jack raised his champagne glass in a mock toast, his lips curving into a smirk. Irina's response was a subtle roll of her eyes before she turned back to the auction, her paddle rising again.

"Thirty million euros!"

A ripple of murmurs coursed through the crowd. The other bidder hesitated, then lowered their paddle in surrender. The auctioneer's gavel struck the podium. "Sold! Lot 47 goes to the lady in black."

Jack watched as Irina's lips curved into the faintest hint of a victorious smile. She turned on her heel, gliding toward the exit, her composure unshaken despite the hefty price tag she'd just dropped. But Jack wasn't about to let her walk out without a word.

He caught up with her just as she reached the elevator leading to the secure area where the artifact was being stored. "Fancy seeing you here," he said, falling into step beside her.

She didn't slow. "Jones. I thought I smelled trouble."

"Funny, I was thinking the same thing. Going solo again? Or is this EISA's idea of diplomacy?"

Her eyes flicked to him, cold and unimpressed. "Stay out of my way. This isn't your operation."

Jack chuckled. "Last I checked, Isaac's syndicate was fair game. Or are you planning to handle this alone?"

"I don't need your help," Irina snapped, her voice as sharp as the stiletto heels clicking on the marble floor.

"Sure you don't," Jack said, falling back slightly as she pressed the elevator button. "But I don't think Isaac's people are going to care about jurisdiction."

The elevator dinged open, and Irina stepped inside, the doors beginning to close between them. Jack lunged forward, slipping inside before she could protest. "I think I'll tag along," he said, flashing her a grin.

Her glare could have melted steel. "If you screw this up—"

"I won't."

The elevator descended, its hum filling the tense silence between them. But before they could reach the storage floor, a sudden explosion rocked the building. The lights flickered, and the elevator jolted to a halt, its emergency brakes screeching as smoke seeped through the seams.

"What the hell was that?" Jack said, bracing himself against the wall.

Irina's hand darted to her thigh, where a concealed blade slipped free of its sheath. "Trouble."

The doors creaked open to reveal chaos. Smoke filled the corridor, and the sound of gunfire echoed in the distance. Two masked men emerged through the haze, their weapons trained on the elevator.

Jack and Irina moved in tandem, their years of training kicking in. Jack lunged for the first gunman, knocking the weapon aside before landing a solid punch to the man's jaw. Irina, meanwhile, disarmed the second with a fluid motion, her blade flashing as she sent him sprawling.

"Not bad," Jack said, his breathing heavy as the gunmen lay unconscious at their feet.

"Save the compliments," Irina snapped, grabbing the artifact's case from a toppled cart nearby. "We need to move."

"Lead the way," Jack said, pulling his pistol from its holster.

Together, they darted through the smoky corridors, the sounds of pursuit growing louder behind them. The artifact was heavier than it looked, its weight pressing down on Irina's hands, but her grip never faltered. Jack covered their rear, his sharp eyes scanning for threats as they wove through the labyrinth of hallways.

"Any bright ideas?" he asked as they rounded a corner, only to find a steel gate blocking their path.

Irina smirked, holding up a keycard she'd lifted during the chaos. "Always."

The gate slid open, and they slipped into the loading bay, where a black SUV sat idling. Jack arched an eyebrow. "Your getaway car?"

Irina shrugged. "Let's just say I came prepared."

They climbed in, and Irina hit the gas, the tires squealing as they sped into the night. Jack glanced at her, his smirk returning. "You know, we make a pretty good team."

She shot him a sidelong look, her expression unreadable. "Don't get used to it."

The SUV vanished into the Zurich streets, leaving the chaos of the auction behind—but neither of them knew just how dangerous the road ahead would become.

CHAPTER 2
A FRAGILE ALLIANCE

THE CHALET PERCHED PRECARIOUSLY on a ridge, blending into the snow-covered forest like a predator in camouflage. Jack Jones surveyed the scene through narrowed eyes as he climbed out of the SUV, his boots crunching against the icy gravel. He glanced over his shoulder at Irina Stepanov, who was already striding toward the cabin door, the artifact cradled securely under one arm.

"Great place for a romantic getaway," Jack muttered, the sarcasm sharp as the cold air biting his skin.

Irina didn't respond, her heels clicking against the stone steps as she swiped a keycard and entered the cabin. Jack followed, still uneasy after the chaotic ambush at the auction.

Inside, the safe house was stark and utilitarian, its warmth barely offsetting the oppressive silence. A stone fireplace dominated one wall, unlit. Surveillance equipment blinked faintly in a corner, monitoring the perimeter.

Irina placed the artifact on the cabin's central table and turned to Jack, her voice as crisp as the alpine air. "We have an hour at most before they find us."

Jack cocked an eyebrow. "Optimistic, aren't we?"

Irina didn't respond immediately. She crossed to the window, her silhouette sharp against the frost-dappled glass, and stared out at the snow-covered forest. Her reflection in the pane was as rigid as her posture. "Optimism isn't a luxury I can afford, Jones," she said at last, her voice quieter. "Not when the stakes are this high."

Jack tilted his head, studying her. "You always this hard on yourself, or is today special?"

"Spare me the psychoanalysis." She pulled her gloves off, one finger at a time, her movements deliberate. But as she tossed them onto the table, her hands lingered, trembling faintly before she clenched them into fists.

Jack opened his mouth, then closed it, unsure whether to press. Irina turned, her usual poise reasserted. "Barricade the windows," she ordered. "I'll deal with the artifact."

Jack crossed his arms, leaning casually against the nearest wall. "I'll help—right after you tell me what's really going on. That thing isn't just a dusty relic, is it?"

Irina shot him a glare. "I don't have time for your theatrics, Jones."

"Humor me," Jack said, his tone hardening. "You bid thirty million euros for it. I'd like to know why."

For a moment, Irina hesitated, then sighed, the fight bleeding from her shoulders. "It's not just an archive. The artifact contains encryption keys tied to Isaac's offshore accounts—financial data he uses to fund his network."

Jack's smirk faded. "And you didn't think to share that earlier?"

"Would you have?" she countered, arching an eyebrow. "Your agency would use the data for their own purposes, just like ours. Don't act like you're above it."

Jack held her gaze, tension crackling between them. "I'm not saying I'm above it. But at least I don't lie about what's at stake."

Irina rolled her eyes and turned back to the artifact, muttering under her breath in Russian as she activated its control panel. Jack's limited understanding of the language didn't help much, but he caught one word clearly: "trouble."

"What's wrong?" he asked, moving to her side.

The small screen on the artifact blinked to life, lines of code scrolling rapidly. Irina's expression darkened. "It's transmitting."

Jack felt a knot tighten in his stomach. "Transmitting what?"

"Coordinates," she said, her voice clipped. "Isaac's people must have embedded a tracking signal. They know we have it."

Meanwhile, deep in his fortified lair, Isaac leaned over a sprawling map of Europe, its surface marked with pins, lines, and coded symbols. A sleek laptop glowed beside him, displaying live feeds from operatives across the globe. His second-in-command, Lucas Brauer, stood nearby, his posture rigid.

"They've compromised Ortega," Brauer said, his clipped German accent sharp.

Isaac didn't look up, his fingers drumming against the map. "Of course they have," he said, almost lazily. "People like Ortega always fold when the stakes get personal." He tapped a finger on a pin marked *Istanbul*. "That's the problem with these agencies. They think loyalty is enough to secure the future."

Brauer hesitated, his eyes narrowing. "And what do you think secures it?"

Karpov's voice broke the silence, his tone clipped as he entered the room. "Blind loyalty doesn't secure the future, that's for sure."

Isaac's eyes flicked to Karpov, his smile thinning. "Careful, Anton. I trust you for your results, not your commentary."

Karpov shrugged, his posture relaxed, but there was a sharpness to his gaze. "Results are why I'm here, and I'm telling you—this Istanbul operation is risky. Too many variables."

"Variables," Isaac repeated, his voice dangerously soft. "Like the ones you failed to account for in Berlin?"

Karpov's jaw tightened, but he held Isaac's gaze. "We got what we needed."

Brauer watched the exchange with quiet interest, his expression unreadable. Isaac finally turned back to the map, dismissing Karpov with a wave. "Ensure Istanbul succeeds, Anton. Or find yourself another employer."

The tension in the room was palpable as Karpov left, his movements precise but deliberate. Brauer waited until the door clicked shut before speaking. "You're losing his loyalty."

Isaac didn't look up. "I don't need his loyalty. I need his obedience."

Isaac straightened, his voice calm but laced with conviction. "Control. The world is chaos, Lucas. Markets collapse, nations betray their allies, and ideologies mean nothing to those who starve. My network brings stability where governments fail. Our methods may be harsh, but our vision is necessary."

"Even if it means war?" Brauer asked, his tone cautious.

Isaac's lips curved into a faint smile. "War is just a tool, Lucas. And tools, when wielded correctly, create order."

Isaac turned away from the table, his gaze falling on the map pinned to the wall. Red lines crisscrossed continents, connecting key locations like veins in a living organism. His hand hovered over the Mediterranean, tracing an invisible path.

"When I was a boy," Isaac began, his voice quieter now, "I watched my father's company collapse. He was a brilliant man, a visionary, but he believed too much in systems—laws, agreements, alliances. When the markets crashed, his partners abandoned him. The structure he'd built turned to dust."

Brauer shifted uncomfortably, his arms crossed. "That was the fault of greed, not order."

Isaac glanced at him, his expression unreadable. "It was the fault of a system too rigid to adapt. Chaos, Lucas—that's where opportunity lies. When the old structures crumble, the clever and the strong don't just survive. They thrive. I saw it then, and I've lived it ever since."

He stepped closer to the map, pinning Brauer with his gaze. "Our work isn't about destruction. It's about evolution. Every bomb, every assassination, every deal—it's the first domino in a chain reaction that leaves something better in its wake."

Brauer didn't reply immediately. When he finally spoke, his voice was cautious. "And what if your chaos spirals out of control?"

Isaac smiled faintly, his confidence unshaken. "Then we guide it. That's why we're here—to ensure the chaos bends to our will."

Jack swore under his breath, running a hand through his hair. "So we've got a homing beacon on us. Fantastic."

Irina's fingers danced over the controls, her jaw tight. "If I can disable it—"

A sudden beep cut her off. The screen flashed red, displaying a single word: Inbound.

Jack grabbed his pistol from his holster. "Too late. They're already on their way."

CHAPTER 3
WEB OF INFLUENCE

THE SPRAWLING GRANDEUR of Vienna's Rathaus was a stark contrast to the smoky chaos of Zurich. Underneath its towering Gothic spires, a glittering fundraiser unfolded, cloaked in the guise of cultural philanthropy. Inside, the hall was a kaleidoscope of chandeliers, champagne flutes, and whispered deals—just another evening in the shadowy world of international influence.

Jack Jones adjusted the lapel of his tuxedo as he stepped out of the car, his eyes scanning the opulent scene with practiced ease. The invitation in his hand bore the name of a wealthy American diplomat, an identity NESA had borrowed for the evening.

Beside him, Irina Stepanov glided across the cobblestones, her black silk gown flowing like liquid shadow. Her poise was unshakable, but Jack sensed the tension beneath her polished exterior. The artifact, now secured in a hidden location, had bought them time—but not much.

"Don't look so tense," Jack said as they approached the entrance. "It's just another party."

Irina's gaze didn't waver as she handed her invitation to the host. "In my experience, parties like this are where the most dangerous games are played."

Jack chuckled under his breath. "And here I thought you liked danger."

The corners of her lips twitched, but she said nothing, her focus already shifting to the crowd ahead.

THE BALLROOM WAS a masterpiece of opulence, its vaulted ceilings painted with scenes from Vienna's imperial past. Diplomats, financiers, and political players milled about, their movements as choreographed as a waltz. At the center of it all was Senator Harold Cartwright, their target.

Cartwright was every bit the archetypal politician—slicked-back hair, an easy smile, and a presence that dominated the room. But behind the charm was a man funding Isaac's operations under the guise of charitable donations.

"There he is," Irina murmured, her green eyes narrowing as she nodded toward Cartwright. "We need to make contact."

Jack nodded, his gaze sweeping the room. "We'll have to be careful. Half this crowd probably has ties to Isaac."

Irina smirked. "Then we fit right in."

As they approached Cartwright, Irina's attention wavered, her gaze locking onto Katerina Ivanov across the room. Memories of their last encounter surged—Katerina's cold smile, the sound of her betrayal ringing in Irina's ears.

"Focus, Stepanov," Jack muttered, his voice pulling her back to the present.

Irina exhaled slowly, forcing herself to smile as they greeted Cartwright. She maintained her composure through the pleasantries, her voice steady even as her pulse thundered in her ears. But the weight of Katerina's presence pressed on her, threatening to crack her carefully crafted façade.

As Cartwright turned to greet another guest, Irina took a step toward Katerina, her fists clenching at her sides. Jack grabbed her arm, his voice low. "What are you doing?"

"I can't let her walk away again," Irina hissed, her voice trembling with suppressed emotion.

"This isn't the time," Jack said, his tone firm. "We're here for Cartwright, remember?"

Irina wavered, the temptation to confront Katerina warring with the logic of Jack's words. Finally, she nodded, her jaw tightening. "This isn't over," she whispered, her voice like steel.

As they approached Cartwright again, Jack adjusted his demeanor, his easygoing charm slipping into place. "Senator Cartwright," he said, extending a hand, "a pleasure to finally meet you. Jack Daniels—of the Daniels family."

Cartwright's smile widened as he shook Jack's hand. "Ah, the Daniels family. Always generous benefactors to a good cause."

"Only the best causes," Jack replied smoothly, motioning to Irina. "And this is my partner, Irina. She's a cultural ambassador."

Irina's smile was as sharp as a blade. "Senator. It's an honor."

"The honor's mine," Cartwright said, his eyes lingering on her for a beat too long. "I've heard Vienna's art scene owes much of its success to collaborations with the Russian Federation."

Irina's smile tightened, but she nodded graciously. "We value collaboration."

For the next thirty minutes, Jack and Irina played their roles perfectly, weaving through the crowd and dropping subtle hints to gauge Cartwright's reactions. Jack kept the conversation light, drawing the senator into anecdotes about his alleged family's wealth, while Irina maneuvered the discussion toward international charities.

Finally, Irina caught Cartwright's arm as he turned to greet another guest. "Senator, a word?"

Jack raised his glass, slipping away to give them space. He positioned himself near a column, his attention divided between keeping an eye on Irina and watching the room for potential threats. Across the ballroom, Cartwright leaned in as Irina spoke, his expression shifting from amusement to intrigue.

Jack's triumph was short-lived. As he started toward them, a hand clamped down on his shoulder. Turning, he came face to face with Anton Karpov, his sharp blue eyes colder than the champagne chilling in the nearby buckets.

"Jones," Karpov said, his voice smooth but carrying an edge. "You've developed a habit of showing up where you don't belong."

Jack masked his surprise with a smirk. "What can I say? I enjoy crashing parties."

Karpov's lips twitched in a semblance of a smile, but his grip didn't loosen. "And yet, you always seem to forget the consequences." He leaned closer, his voice lowering. "Walk away from this, Jones. Whatever you think you're accomplishing here, it's not worth the price."

"And what price is that?" Jack asked, his tone casual but his pulse quickening.

"Everything," Karpov replied, his eyes briefly flicking toward Irina and Cartwright. "You think Isaac is the villain here, but the truth is far more complicated. There are powers at play even he doesn't control. Powers you've underestimated."

Jack studied him, the faintest flicker of doubt creeping in. "Since when did you start caring about casualties, Karpov?"

The Russian's smile was thin and humorless. "I don't. But sometimes, a man learns that survival depends on choosing the right moment to step aside."

Across the room, Irina finished her conversation with Cartwright, slipping back toward Jack. She noticed Karpov immediately, her expression tightening as she approached.

"Anton," she said, her voice smooth. "I see you're still freelancing."

"Stepanov," Karpov replied, his tone laced with disdain. "Always meddling where you don't belong."

Irina stepped closer, her gaze icy. "You seem nervous. Afraid I'll ruin your plans again?"

Jack glanced between them, sensing the tension. "As much as I'd love to watch this reunion, we've got somewhere to be."

Karpov's smile faded, his hand brushing against his jacket—a subtle warning. "Be careful, Jones. Not everyone in this room is as charming as me."

With that, he disappeared into the crowd, leaving Jack and Irina alone.

THEY DIDN'T SPEAK until they were outside, the cold night air cutting through the lingering tension.

"What did you get from Cartwright?" Jack asked.

Irina held up a small USB drive. "Enough to confirm his ties to Isaac. Bank accounts, transaction records—it's all there."

Jack nodded, his relief tempered by lingering unease. "And Karpov?"

"He's a problem," Irina admitted. "If he knows we're here, so does Isaac."

Jack's jaw tightened. "Then we'd better stay ahead."

As they climbed into the waiting car, Jack glanced at Irina, his tone softer. "Good work in there."

She met his gaze, her expression unreadable. "Let's hope it's enough."

The car pulled away, the lights of Vienna fading into the distance. For now, they had what they needed—but Jack couldn't shake the feeling that their enemies were closing in faster than they realized.

CHAPTER 4
AN ENEMY WITHIN

THE PRAGUE SKYLINE gleamed under a crescent moon, its Gothic spires and modern skyscrapers blending history and progress. Jack Jones leaned against a crumbling stone parapet overlooking the Vltava River, the soft glow of streetlights reflecting off the water below. In the distance, the hum of the city's nightlife felt like a world apart from the covert operation unfolding in the shadows.

Beside him, Irina Stepanov stood as still as a statue, her gaze fixed on the entrance of a nondescript building. It looked like any other warehouse in the industrial district, but Jack knew better. Inside, Isaac's associates were meeting with someone they couldn't afford to lose—a contact tied to the encrypted files on the USB drive Irina had pulled from Senator Cartwright.

Jack shifted his weight, the tension in his shoulders unfamiliar yet undeniable. "You're quiet tonight," he said, his voice low. "Unusual for you."

Irina didn't look at him. "I don't waste words when there's nothing to say."

Jack smirked, but it was more out of habit than ease. He glanced at the dark water of the Vltava below, his reflection fractured by the ripples. "You ever think about what happens when this is over?" His tone was casual, but the question lingered between them like smoke.

Irina turned to him briefly, her green eyes narrowing. "Over? You're more naïve than I thought."

Jack didn't respond immediately. He watched the reflection fade before straightening. "Fair enough," he muttered, though her words hit closer than he cared to admit. Maybe Irina was right—this wasn't the kind of life you walked away from. Still, some part of him clung to the faint hope that when Isaac's shadow fell, there'd be light on the other side.

She turned to him, her green eyes glinting in the moonlight. "You're right. I don't."

BEFORE JACK COULD RESPOND, his earpiece crackled. "Jones, Stepanov— movement inside," Director Farrow's voice came through faintly. "A convoy just pulled up. Looks like Isaac's people are here."

Jack straightened, his hand brushing the pistol holstered under his jacket. "Showtime."

They slipped from the parapet and moved toward the warehouse's side entrance, sticking to the shadows. The air smelled of oil and rust, every sound amplified by the stillness. Jack could feel the tension radiating from Irina as they crept closer.

"I'll take point," Irina said, her voice barely audible.

Jack frowned. "What happened to teamwork?"

"I prefer efficiency."

Before he could argue, she was already moving, her steps silent on the cracked pavement. Jack followed, his frustration tempered by a grudging admiration for her precision. Inside, the warehouse was dark except for the glow of a few overhead lamps illuminating a cluster of figures near the center.

JACK AND IRINA crouched behind a stack of crates, their eyes locked on the group. Three men flanked a tall figure in a tailored suit—Lucas Brauer, one of Isaac's top lieutenants. Opposite him stood a woman with short-cropped hair and a commanding presence. Jack recognized her immediately.

"Maria Ortega," he whispered. "EISA's regional director."

Irina's sharp intake of breath betrayed her shock. "What is she doing here?"

Jack's jaw tightened. "Looks like your agency has some explaining to do."

Irina's gaze didn't waver as she studied the scene. "Ortega's been overseeing EISA operations in Central Europe for years. If she's working with Isaac—"

"Then she's selling out your entire agency," Jack finished grimly. "What's the plan?"

For a moment, Irina hesitated. Then her expression hardened. "We wait. If we move now, we risk blowing our cover."

As they waited, the faint sound of Brauer's voice drifted from the center of the warehouse. Jack glanced at Irina, but her focus was locked on the scene ahead.

"You trust him?" Jack whispered, nodding toward Karpov, who stood near the edge of the group, his posture tense but watchful.

Irina's expression didn't waver. "No. But I trust his ambition. Karpov doesn't follow Isaac out of loyalty. He follows him because he thinks he can control the chaos better."

Jack smirked. "Sounds familiar."

Irina's lips tightened. "The difference is, I know when to walk away. Karpov will hold onto Isaac's coattails until the whole system collapses—or until he thinks he can take over."

Jack's gaze shifted back to the group, his voice low. "Let's make sure he doesn't get the chance."

Jack opened his mouth to argue, but the sound of raised voices drew their attention back to the meeting. Ortega was holding a tablet, the screen glowing as she handed it to Brauer. He examined it, nodding in satisfaction.

"This confirms the transfer," Brauer said, his German accent clipped. "Isaac will be pleased."

Ortega smiled, but it didn't reach her eyes. "Tell him to hold up his

end of the deal. If these accounts are exposed, my position becomes...
untenable."

Jack's stomach churned. "She's covering her tracks."

Irina's lips pressed into a thin line. "We need to stop this."

BEFORE JACK COULD RESPOND, a sudden crash echoed through the warehouse as one of the crates toppled over. The sound drew the attention of Brauer's men, who immediately raised their weapons.

"Who's there?" Brauer barked, his hand hovering near his holster.

Jack swore under his breath. "So much for stealth."

He and Irina emerged from their hiding spot, their weapons drawn. "Drop it, Brauer," Jack said, his voice steady. "We just want the files."

Brauer sneered. "And who are you to demand anything?"

"I'm the guy with a gun pointed at your head," Jack replied. "Your move."

Ortega stepped forward, her expression unreadable. "Agent Stepanov," she said, ignoring Jack. "This is a misunderstanding. Lower your weapon, and we can discuss this."

Irina didn't budge. "A misunderstanding? You're working with Isaac."

"Don't be naïve," Ortega snapped. "The data on that drive could destabilize half of Europe if it gets into the wrong hands. EISA has made arrangements to ensure stability."

Irina's glare intensified, but Ortega met it head-on, her expression unyielding. "You think I enjoy this?" Ortega asked, her voice rising. "Do you have any idea how many fires I've put out in the past decade? How many disasters I've averted by aligning with people like Isaac?"

"And how many innocents have you sacrificed along the way?" Irina shot back, her tone icy.

Ortega's jaw tightened. "Sometimes, sacrifices are unavoidable. What EISA does—what I do—isn't clean or easy. But without us, there would be no stability. No balance." Her voice dropped, thick with emotion. "I've made choices I'll carry to my grave, Stepanov. But at least I'll know I did what was necessary."

Irina's voice softened, just barely. "And how long before Isaac turns on you, Ortega? How long before your choices destroy the very stability you're clinging to?"

Ortega faltered, but only for a moment. "That's a risk I'm willing to take."

"By funding a criminal empire?" Irina shot back, her voice icy. "You've crossed the line."

Jack kept his focus on Brauer, but his mind raced. Ortega's betrayal was deeper than they'd suspected. If Irina didn't act fast, they'd lose their chance to expose her.

THE TENSION WAS razor-sharp as Ortega raised her hands, her tone softening. "Irina, listen to me. We're on the same side."

"No," Irina said, her voice steady. "We're not."

The shot rang out before Jack could react. Irina's bullet hit Ortega's tablet, shattering the screen and sending the device clattering to the floor. Brauer's men opened fire, forcing Jack and Irina to dive behind the crates.

"You always have to make things complicated," Jack muttered as he returned fire.

Irina didn't respond, her focus locked on the chaos ahead. One by one, they took down Brauer's men, the firefight echoing through the warehouse. When the dust settled, Brauer and Ortega were gone, the faint sound of an engine signaling their escape.

JACK LEANED AGAINST THE CRATES, catching his breath. "Well, that went great."

Irina retrieved the shattered remains of Ortega's tablet, her expression grim. "We have enough evidence to implicate her. Brauer confirmed the transfer."

"Good luck getting EISA to believe you," Jack said, his tone laced with bitterness. "They'll protect her if it means saving face."

"Then I'll make them believe," Irina said, her voice cold. "This isn't over."

Jack watched her, a flicker of respect breaking through his frustration. "You're relentless, I'll give you that."

"It's the only way to win," she replied, turning toward the exit. "Let's go. We've got work to do."

As they disappeared into the Prague night, Jack couldn't shake the feeling that the battle was far from over. Ortega's betrayal was just the beginning, and Isaac's shadow loomed larger than ever.

CHAPTER 5
THE MISSION AT THE EMBASSY

THE GALA at the French Embassy in Berlin was as opulent as one would expect. Crystal chandeliers bathed the room in golden light, their reflections dancing across polished marble floors. Diplomats, dignitaries, and Europe's elite mingled beneath the vaulted ceilings, their laughter and clinking glasses masking the tension thrumming beneath the surface.

Jack Jones adjusted his bow tie, scanning the room with the relaxed air of a man enjoying the finest the city had to offer. Yet his sharp eyes missed nothing, registering every movement and shadowed conversation.

"You look almost convincing," Irina Stepanov murmured as she stepped up beside him, her black gown shimmering under the lights. Her voice was smooth, but her eyes betrayed her focus. "Almost."

Jack smirked, sipping his champagne. "You don't have to be jealous, Stepanov. Some of us were born to blend in."

She arched an eyebrow, unimpressed. "If by blending in, you mean drawing attention to yourself, then yes, you're doing an excellent job."

Jack chuckled but didn't take the bait. Instead, he glanced across the room at their target: Dimitri Valenko. The young Russian operative sat at a table near the far wall, his posture stiff as he sipped from a glass of red wine. Even from a distance, his unease was palpable.

Dimitri's handlers were discreet but not invisible. Two men lingered near the bar, their gazes flicking toward him every few seconds. Another stood near the exit, his hand resting casually inside his jacket.

"This won't be easy," Jack muttered. "He's being watched."

Irina nodded, her expression unreadable. "That's why we stick to the plan."

Jack's smirk faltered. "About that—are you sure this is going to work?"

She fixed him with a level stare. "Do you have a better idea?"

Jack opened his mouth, then closed it again. He didn't. As much as he hated to admit it, Irina's plan—faking an assassination attempt on Dimitri to force him into their custody—was their best shot at getting him out alive.

MOVING WITH PRACTICED EASE, Jack and Irina split up, each blending into the crowd. Jack approached the bar, ordering a scotch as he kept a casual eye on Dimitri's handlers. Irina circled the room, her presence subtle but deliberate as she positioned herself near their target.

Farrow's voice crackled in Jack's earpiece. "Jones, do you copy?"

"Loud and clear," Jack murmured, his lips barely moving. "We're in position."

"Good. This has to go off without a hitch. Dimitri's intel is the only lead we have on Isaac's next move."

"No pressure," Jack replied dryly, his gaze flicking toward Irina. She stood just behind Dimitri now, her expression calm as she pretended to admire a nearby painting.

A waiter passed by with a tray of champagne, and Irina slipped something into one of the glasses—a fast-acting sedative designed to mimic the symptoms of poisoning. She picked up the glass and offered it to Dimitri with a warm smile.

"For the guest of honor," she said, her voice light.

Dimitri hesitated, his eyes narrowing as he studied her. "I don't believe we've met."

"Irina Stepanov," she replied smoothly. "A friend of a friend. You've made quite an impression tonight."

Dimitri's suspicion lingered for a moment longer, but then he took the glass, his lips curling into a faint smile. "To impressions, then."

He drank, and Irina stepped away, her movements unhurried as she disappeared into the crowd. Jack watched from the bar, his grip tightening around his glass.

"Phase one complete," Irina's voice came through his earpiece. "He should feel it any second."

———

THE FIRST SIGNS WERE SUBTLE. Dimitri blinked rapidly, his hand trembling slightly as he set his glass down. Then he swayed, his face paling. One of his handlers noticed immediately, rushing to his side.

"Sir? Are you all right?" the man asked, his voice tinged with alarm.

Dimitri didn't answer. His knees buckled, and he collapsed onto the table, sending his wine glass shattering to the floor. The room erupted into chaos as guests gasped and whispered, their attention fixed on the commotion.

Jack moved quickly, slipping through the panicked crowd toward the exit. Irina was already there, her expression composed as she activated her earpiece. "He's down. Let's move."

Dimitri's handlers were distracted, their focus entirely on their fallen charge. As they shouted for medical assistance, Irina signaled to a pair of NESA operatives disguised as embassy staff. The operatives pushed a gurney into the room, intercepting Dimitri before his own people could take him.

"Medical emergency," one of them announced. "We'll handle this."

Jack joined Irina as they slipped out the side door, their pace brisk as they moved toward the waiting van. The operatives followed moments later, wheeling Dimitri out and loading him into the vehicle.

———

THE VAN SPED through Berlin's streets, its interior dimly lit. Dimitri lay on the gurney, his breathing shallow but steady. The sedative would wear off soon, and Jack could already see the signs—his fingers twitching, his eyelids fluttering.

"You sure this was the right play?" Jack asked, his voice low.

Irina glanced at him, her expression cool. "We needed him out of there. Do you have a problem with the result?"

Jack shook his head but didn't respond. Instead, he turned his attention to Dimitri, who let out a low groan as his eyes fluttered open.

"What... what's going on?" Dimitri muttered, his voice slurred.

"Relax," Irina said, leaning forward. "You're safe."

Dimitri's gaze sharpened as recognition dawned. "You... you poisoned me."

"We saved you," Jack corrected, his tone firm. "Isaac's people were using you. We're giving you a way out."

Dimitri laughed bitterly, his head lolling against the gurney. "There's no way out. Not with Isaac."

"There is," Irina said, her voice steady. "But you need to trust us."

Dimitri's eyes narrowed. "Why should I?"

Jack leaned closer, his tone sharp. "Because if we wanted you dead, you wouldn't be here. Now start talking. What's Isaac planning?"

For a moment, Dimitri hesitated, his eyes flicking between them. Then he exhaled, his shoulders sagging. "He's targeting the UN Summit. It's... it's all in the files."

"What files?" Irina pressed.

Dimitri swallowed hard. "Encrypted files. Hidden at his safe house in Marseille."

Jack exchanged a glance with Irina, their unspoken agreement clear. This was their next move.

As THE VAN disappeared into Berlin's outskirts, Jack couldn't shake the feeling that the stakes had just climbed higher than ever. Dimitri's intel was a lead, but it was also a trap—one that Isaac would have prepared for.

Beside him, Irina sat in silence, her focus unbroken. For now, they were one step ahead. But Jack knew better than to think it would last.

CHAPTER 6
INTO THE DEN

THE RUGGED CLIFFS of Marseille's coastline loomed against the dawn, jagged and unyielding as the waves crashed below. Nestled into the rocky terrain was Isaac's rumored safe house—a sleek, modern fortress of glass and steel overlooking the Mediterranean. To the untrained eye, it looked like the retreat of a wealthy recluse. Jack Jones knew better.

"This place screams 'come and get me,'" Jack muttered, adjusting the night-vision goggles perched on his face. He crouched behind a cluster of boulders with Irina Stepanov, the predawn chill biting through their black tactical gear.

"Because it's a trap," Irina replied, her voice clipped. She scanned the safe house through binoculars, her green eyes sharp as she tracked the movement of armed guards patrolling the perimeter. "Isaac knows we're coming."

"Which begs the question," Jack said, glancing at her, "why are we still here?"

Irina lowered the binoculars, her expression steely. "Because Dimitri's intel points here. If Isaac's files are inside, we can't afford to leave empty-handed."

Jack sighed, shaking his head. "You're relentless. I'll give you that."

"Flattery won't save you," she said without missing a beat. "Stick to the plan."

THE PLAN, as usual, was straightforward on paper and chaotic in execution. Using the cliffside's shadows as cover, they approached the safe house from the west, where the guards' patrol routes overlapped the least. Jack kept his pistol ready, his steps light against the gravel path. Irina moved ahead of him, her knife glinting faintly as she neutralized the first guard with a swift, silent takedown.

"Still enjoying the quiet approach?" Jack whispered as they slipped past the unconscious man.

"It's called subtlety, Jones," she shot back. "You should try it sometime."

They reached the outer wall, a sleek expanse of steel and bullet-proof glass. Irina pulled a compact device from her pouch, attaching it to the electronic lock on a side door. The device hummed faintly as it worked to override the system.

"Let me guess," Jack said, keeping watch. "EISA tech?"

Irina didn't look up. "Do you want to compare gadgets or get inside?"

Jack smirked but said nothing as the lock clicked open. Irina pushed the door gently, slipping inside with Jack close behind.

THE INTERIOR WAS as cold and calculated as Isaac's reputation—bare walls, minimal furniture, and an air of sterile precision. The faint hum of security cameras filled the silence, their lenses sweeping the hallways.

Irina held up a hand, signaling Jack to stop. She knelt beside a narrow panel in the floor, her fingers tracing the edges. With a flick of her wrist, she pried it open, revealing a network of wires.

As she worked, Jack crouched beside her, his curiosity outweighing his usual restraint. "You're good at this," he said, his voice low. "Let me guess—something you picked up at EISA?"

Irina's fingers stilled for half a second before resuming. "Not EISA. Before that."

Jack raised an eyebrow. "Before that?"

She didn't look at him, but her voice softened, the precision of her movements matched by the deliberate cadence of her words. "I grew up in Moscow. My father was… resourceful. Always working angles, always watching for threats. He taught me to see the world as it is— layers of deception and opportunity." Her tone hardened. "But when his angle got him killed, I learned to stop relying on anyone but myself."

Jack watched her, the lines between them shifting. "And now you work for an agency built on deception."

She looked at him then, her green eyes unflinching. "We all make compromises, Jones. What matters is that we make them for the right reasons."

The camera system powered down with a faint click. Irina stood, brushing dust from her hands. "Let's move."

THE FILES WERE STORED in a high-security vault on the lower level. The elevator was a nonstarter, so they took the stairs, their footsteps muffled by sound-dampening soles. At the bottom, they encountered two more guards. Jack gestured for Irina to stay back as he crept forward, his movements fluid and silent.

The first guard went down with a swift blow to the neck. The second turned too late, Jack's elbow connecting with his jaw. He dragged the unconscious bodies into the shadows before motioning for Irina to follow.

"You're welcome," Jack said, flashing her a grin.

She rolled her eyes but didn't respond, already focused on the vault door ahead. It was reinforced steel, its keypad glowing faintly in the dim light.

"This will take time," Irina murmured, pulling out yet another device. "Keep watch."

Jack positioned himself near the stairwell, his pistol raised. The seconds dragged on, each one marked by the distant hum of the building's security system. Then, a faint beep signaled the vault's release.

"Got it," Irina said, pulling the door open.

Inside, rows of locked drawers lined the walls, each labeled with a cryptic code. Irina moved with purpose, locating the drawer Dimitri's intel had identified. She inserted a slim tool into the lock, twisting it until the mechanism clicked.

The drawer slid open, revealing a set of encrypted hard drives. Irina's lips curved into a rare, satisfied smile.

"Bingo," she said, slipping the drives into her pack.

As Irina zipped the pack shut, a faint chime echoed through the room. Jack tensed, his pistol raising instinctively, but it wasn't an alarm —it was the vault's intercom system, crackling to life.

"Agent Jones," Isaac's voice drawled through the speakers, calm and unhurried. "So predictable. Did you think I wouldn't notice you sniffing around my operations?"

Jack froze, his grip tightening on the pistol. Isaac's voice continued, smooth as silk. "I must admit, I've grown quite fond of your work, Jack. You're a man who values loyalty—even if it's to ghosts."

The words hit like a blow, and Jack's jaw clenched. "What the hell do you know about loyalty?"

"Oh, I know plenty. Like how loyalty to your sister kept you grounded after Munich. What was her name again? Amy?"

Jack's blood ran cold, his mind flashing to the photo he carried in his wallet. "You leave her out of this."

Isaac chuckled, a low, mocking sound. "Relax. She's safe. For now. But you might want to consider whether meddling in my affairs is worth the risk to her charming little family."

Irina shot Jack a warning glance, her voice low. "We need to go. Now."

Jack didn't move, his chest heaving as Isaac's words echoed in his head. Finally, he turned to Irina, his voice taut. "Get the drives. We end this."

THE ALARM SOUNDED the moment they stepped out of the vault. Red lights bathed the hallway as the building's automated security system activated.

"Guess your fancy gadgets didn't catch everything," Jack said, running alongside Irina as they headed for the stairs.

"I don't need a lecture right now," she snapped, her pistol drawn.

They reached the ground floor as guards swarmed the building, their shouts echoing through the halls. Jack fired off a few shots, his aim precise as he covered Irina's advance.

"Window," she shouted, pointing to a large pane of reinforced glass overlooking the cliffs.

"You're kidding," Jack said, but the look on her face told him she wasn't.

Together, they fired at the glass until it shattered, the sound of breaking shards barely audible over the alarm. Without hesitation, Irina leapt through, landing in a roll on the rocky ground outside. Jack followed, wincing as the jagged terrain bit into his hands and knees.

They scrambled toward the cliff's edge, where a zipline was anchored to a steel post. Irina clipped on first, sliding into the darkness with practiced ease. Jack followed, his heart racing as the wind whipped past him.

They landed on a secluded beach below, the roar of the waves masking the distant shouts of their pursuers. A small motorboat waited at the water's edge, its engine idling.

Irina climbed aboard, her movements efficient. "Get in," she said, not looking back.

Jack obeyed, collapsing onto the seat beside her as the boat sped away. He glanced at her, his breath still coming in short bursts. "That was insane."

"It worked," she replied, her tone cool. "Now let's see what Isaac was hiding."

As the coastline faded into the distance, Jack couldn't shake the feeling that they'd only just begun to unravel Isaac's web. The hard drives were a victory, but the war was far from over.

CHAPTER 7
TRUST TESTED

THE SAFE HOUSE in Istanbul was a stark departure from Marseille's high-tech fortress. Hidden in the bustling heart of the city, it was a modest apartment tucked above a spice shop. The scent of cardamom and saffron drifted through the cracked windows as Jack Jones sat at a small wooden table, his eyes fixed on the encrypted hard drives Irina Stepanov had retrieved.

Across the room, Irina was typing on a laptop, her green eyes sharp with concentration. Her demeanor was as unyielding as ever, but Jack could see the cracks—the faint tension in her shoulders, the subtle way her fingers trembled when she thought no one was watching.

"You're going to wear out the keyboard," Jack quipped, breaking the silence.

Irina didn't look up. "Some of us don't waste time making jokes when there's work to be done."

Jack leaned back in his chair, folding his arms. "And some of us know when to breathe. You've been glued to that thing for hours. What's the rush?"

Irina's fingers paused, and she fixed him with a sharp look. "This isn't a game, Jones. Every second we waste, Isaac gets closer to destabilizing entire regions. People will die if we're too slow."

Jack raised an eyebrow, his tone sardonic. "And you think running yourself into the ground is going to stop him? Hate to break it to you, but you're not invincible."

Her glare was like ice. "And you think I don't know that? Every choice we make has consequences, Jones. People die either way. But if working myself to exhaustion saves even one innocent life, then it's worth it."

Jack's smirk faded, and he leaned forward, his voice lowering. "But what happens when you're the one who needs saving? What happens when the lines you cross blur so much you can't find your way back?"

Irina looked away, her lips pressing into a thin line. "There's no way back for people like us. You know that as well as I do."

She sighed, her fingers pausing on the keys. "The sooner we decrypt these files, the sooner we know what Isaac's planning."

"And the sooner we figure out why your agency's covering for him," Jack added, his tone pointed.

Irina's jaw tightened. "This isn't about EISA."

"Isn't it?" Jack stood, pacing the small room. "First Ortega, now Dimitri's files pointing to your agency's involvement. Face it, Stepanov —EISA's neck-deep in this." He stopped, hands on his hips, a bitter laugh escaping. "And I'm neck-deep in trusting you to tell me the truth. Great team we make, huh?"

Irina's glare didn't waver, but Jack caught the flicker of something beneath her armor—guilt, maybe. It was enough to pull him up short. He exhaled, running a hand over his face. "Look, I'm not accusing you of anything," he said, softer now. "But it feels like every step we take, there's another twist—another game someone's playing with our lives."

Irina hesitated, her lips parting as though to respond. Then she closed her mouth, turning back to the laptop. "This isn't a game, Jones. Not for me."

She typed faster, the tension in her movements betraying the calm she tried to project. "You want to know why I don't talk about trust, Jones? Because it's a luxury. And luxuries get people killed."

Jack tilted his head, his tone softening. "That what happened to you? Someone broke your trust?"

Irina froze, her fingers hovering over the keyboard. For a moment, Jack thought she wouldn't answer. Then she sighed, her voice barely above a whisper. "It was my first year at EISA. I recruited a woman named Katerina Ivanov—brilliant, loyal... or so I thought. She wasn't just an analyst; she was a friend. I vouched for her, trained her, trusted her."

Jack leaned forward, his curiosity tempered by the pain he saw flicker in her eyes. "What happened?"

Irina's jaw tightened. "She sold agency secrets to Isaac. Dozens of operatives were compromised—some killed—because of her. And I didn't see it coming. I didn't want to see it. I believed her, right up until the moment I confronted her and she put a gun to my head."

The silence that followed was heavy, broken only by the faint hum of the laptop. Jack rubbed the back of his neck, unsure what to say. "So, no more trust."

Irina's laugh was bitter. "No more illusions, Jones. It's the only way to survive."

Her gaze snapped to him, cold and unyielding. "Don't pretend NESA is any better. Your agency has skeletons in its closet too."

Jack stopped pacing, his eyes locking onto hers. "Maybe. But right now, those skeletons aren't funding a global crime syndicate."

THE TENSION WAS INTERRUPTED by a sudden buzz from the laptop. Irina's fingers flew across the keyboard as lines of code scrolled across the screen.

"It's decrypting," she said, her voice tight with focus.

Jack moved to her side, his sharp eyes scanning the data as it began to resolve into legible files. Names, bank accounts, and transaction records filled the screen, each line painting a clearer picture of Isaac's operation.

"Look at this," Irina murmured, pointing to a series of deposits. "Massive amounts of money flowing into shell accounts in Hong Kong, Zurich, and Dubai."

Jack frowned. "All tied to arms shipments."

Irina clicked on another file, her expression darkening. "And this—Isaac's next move. He's targeting an arms deal in Istanbul."

Jack's stomach sank as he read the details. The deal was set to take place in less than twelve hours, and the buyers weren't just low-level criminals—they were rogue agents from multiple intelligence agencies.

"This isn't just about weapons," Jack said, his voice grim. "Isaac's selling influence—access to the kind of firepower that can destabilize entire regions."

Irina nodded, her face pale but determined. "We have to stop it."

Jack's earpiece buzzed with Farrow's voice. "Intercept them at the monastery. Dimitri's intel says that's where the buyer will confirm the deal."

Irina raised an eyebrow. "A monastery? Isaac's got a flair for theatrics."

Jack grinned. "You'd get along."

THE MONASTERY CLUNG to a jagged cliff, its ancient stone walls shrouded in mist. As they ascended the winding path, the air grew colder, the wind howling like a warning. Jack scanned the area, noting the guards stationed at key points, their rifles incongruous against the serene backdrop.

"Peaceful," he muttered. "Bet the monks are thrilled."

Inside, the central chamber was vast and echoing, its high ceilings adorned with faded frescoes. At the center, Isaac's operatives stood in a loose semicircle, flanking the buyer—a sharp-dressed woman with a briefcase. Jack and Irina hid behind a stone pillar, watching as the negotiation unfolded.

"Ten million euros now," the buyer said, her tone clipped. "The rest when delivery is confirmed." She opened the briefcase to reveal rows of neatly stacked cash.

Isaac's lieutenant smirked, his hand resting on the handle of a large, metal case. "No trust in my word?"

"In your business, trust is just another currency," the buyer replied.

Jack leaned toward Irina. "We need to get that case."

Irina's green eyes sparkled with determination. "Follow my lead."

She stepped into the open, her pistol raised. "Everyone freeze."

The operatives reacted instantly, drawing their weapons. But Irina's voice cut through the tension. "Do you really want to test your luck in a building with three-foot-thick stone walls? Because I don't think bullets are your friends here."

The buyer tilted her head, intrigued. "And who might you be?"

"Someone who can double what you're paying—for the right information," Irina replied smoothly, lowering her weapon slightly.

Jack suppressed a smirk. Classic Stepanov. As the buyer hesitated, he circled behind the group, his footsteps silent against the stone floor.

"That's a bold claim," the buyer said, her eyes narrowing.

Irina smiled coldly. "Try me."

At that moment, Jack lunged, grabbing the metal case. Chaos erupted as shots rang out, ricocheting off the ancient walls. Monks emerged from hidden corridors, their chants turning into cries of alarm. Jack and Irina fought their way out, the case clutched tightly between them as the operatives gave chase.

AS THEY PREPARED TO LEAVE, Jack hesitated, his gaze lingering on Irina. "You sure you're up for this?"

She stiffened. "I don't need your concern, Jones."

"It's not concern," Jack replied. "It's caution. If there's a mole in EISA, you could be walking into a trap."

Irina turned to face him, her eyes blazing. "And you think I don't know that? You think I haven't considered every possibility?"

"I think you're too focused on proving yourself to see the bigger picture," Jack said, his tone softer now. "We're supposed to be a team, remember?"

Irina's shoulders sagged slightly, the fight draining from her. "Trust doesn't come easily in this world, Jack."

He offered a faint smile. "No kidding. But if we don't trust each other, we're dead."

She didn't respond, but the flicker of vulnerability in her eyes was answer enough.

CHAPTER 8
ROGUE MOVES

BERLIN'S LIGHTS shimmered through the penthouse windows, illuminating Jack Jones as he leaned over a table strewn with maps, schematics, and the contents of the flash drive he had recovered in Istanbul. The faint hum of the city below served as a distant backdrop to the storm brewing in the room.

"Got something," Irina Stepanov announced from across the room. She was perched on the edge of a desk, her laptop casting a pale glow across her face. "The flash drive's metadata points to a gala tomorrow night. One of Isaac's high-level operatives will be there."

Jack frowned, circling the table. "You think it's the same operative who slipped out of Istanbul?"

Irina nodded, her expression tight. "The timing fits. She's likely tying Isaac's arms deals to his political backers. If we get to her, we get everything."

Jack smirked. "Sounds like a plan."

"Not quite," Irina said, standing. "She'll have security—layers of it. This isn't a smash-and-grab. We'll need to blend in."

Jack raised an eyebrow. "You mean dress up and play nice with people who'd rather see us dead? Sounds fun."

Irina's lips curved into a faint smile. "Then try not to embarrass yourself."

THE GRAND BALLROOM at Berlin's Altes Museum was a masterpiece of classical architecture, its marble columns and gilded accents exuding timeless elegance. Jack adjusted the cuffs of his tuxedo, his movements deliberate as he scanned the crowd. The weight of the small pistol holstered beneath his jacket was a comforting presence.

For a moment, Jack let his eyes drift beyond the glittering crowd. The grandeur of the Altes Museum, its towering columns and gilded chandeliers, felt alien yet familiar—a stark contrast to the cramped safe houses and shadowy alleyways he'd called home for years.

He remembered being a fresh recruit, wide-eyed and eager, believing in the romance of espionage. The tuxedos, the high-stakes conversations, the promise of saving the world one covert mission at a time. But the years had stripped away the glamour, leaving only the cold, relentless grind of the job.

"You look almost convincing," Irina murmured, pulling him from his thoughts. Her voice was smooth, but her eyes betrayed her focus. "Almost."

Jack smirked, the spell broken. "I clean up nice, don't I?"

Irina entered moments later, and for a second, Jack forgot to breathe. She wore a sleek, emerald-green gown that caught the light as she moved, her hair swept into a simple yet elegant twist. She was the picture of poise and danger.

"Try to focus, Jones," she murmured as she slipped her arm through his. "We're on the clock."

Jack cleared his throat, his smirk returning. "I'm focused. You clean up well, by the way."

"Flattery will get you nowhere," she replied, her eyes scanning the room.

Their target—a tall woman with short-cropped hair—stood near the edge of the room, deep in conversation with two men in tailored suits. Jack recognized one of them as a well-known arms dealer tied to Isaac's syndicate.

"There she is," Irina murmured. "Katerina Ivanov."

"Any idea how we're getting her alone?" Jack asked.

Irina's smile was sharp. "Leave that to me."

IRINA BROKE AWAY FROM JACK, weaving through the crowd with the confidence of someone who belonged. At the bar, she slipped into Katerina Ivanov's orbit, her timing impeccable.

"Katerina Ivanov," Irina said warmly, as though greeting an old friend. "It's an honor to finally meet you."

Katerina's sharp eyes narrowed. "And who might you be?"

"Natasha Kuznetsova," Irina replied smoothly, her Russian accent flawless. "I represent an investment group interested in your ventures. Perhaps we could discuss?"

Katerina hesitated, then nodded, her curiosity piqued. "Lead the way."

Irina caught Jack's eye as they passed, giving him the faintest nod.

Jack moved to intercept Katerina's companions, engaging them in a feigned drunken conversation that kept their attention diverted. It bought Irina the time she needed.

IN A SECLUDED CORNER, Katerina leaned against the wall, her glass of champagne glinting in the dim light. "So, Natasha, what exactly do you want to discuss?"

Irina's smile didn't reach her eyes. "I'd like to know about Isaac's plans for the UN Summit."

Katerina's hand froze on her glass, her expression hardening. "I think you're mistaken."

"I don't think I am," Irina said, her voice low. "You've been moving weapons, funding proxies, and buying influence. Whatever Isaac is planning, it's about to get a lot of people killed."

Katerina's jaw tightened, her free hand edging toward her purse. "You're playing a dangerous game."

Irina stepped closer, her voice ice-cold. "So are you. But I don't play to lose."

Katerina moved suddenly, pulling a small knife from her purse. Irina was faster, grabbing Katerina's wrist and twisting it until the knife clattered to the floor.

"You're going to tell me everything," Irina said, her grip unyielding. "Or I'll make sure you disappear before dessert."

BEFORE KATERINA COULD RESPOND, a commotion erupted near the entrance. Jack turned, his hand instinctively moving to his pistol as two men in tactical gear stormed into the ballroom. The crowd panicked, screams echoing as guests scattered.

"Looks like Isaac's people crashed the party," Jack muttered into his earpiece. "Irina, status?"

"I'm with Katerina," she replied. "She's not talking."

"Then we improvise," Jack said, making his way toward her location.

Katerina struggled against Irina's grip, her fear giving way to desperation. "You think you can just walk out of here? They'll kill you both."

Irina smirked. "Let them try."

Jack arrived just as Irina pulled Katerina toward a side door. "I hope you've got an exit plan," he said.

"Always," Irina replied, pushing Katerina ahead of them.

THE SIDE DOOR led to an alley, where a black SUV idled with its engine running. Jack and Irina climbed in, shoving Katerina between them as the driver sped off.

"Talk," Irina ordered, her tone sharp.

Katerina hesitated, her defiance crumbling under Irina's unflinching stare. "Isaac's using the UN Summit to destabilize Europe. He's planning coordinated attacks on major cities to trigger panic and collapse the economy."

Jack swore under his breath. "And where's the command center?"

Katerina's voice wavered. "A private yacht in the Adriatic. He's keeping his inner circle there until it's over."

Irina exchanged a glance with Jack, their unspoken agreement clear. This was their next target.

As the SUV disappeared into Berlin's streets, Jack leaned back, his mind racing. The stakes had never been higher, and the margin for error was razor-thin.

"Looks like we're going to need a boat," he said, his voice laced with grim humor.

Irina didn't smile, her focus unbroken. "This isn't over."

Jack nodded, his gaze shifting to the window. "Not even close."

CHAPTER 9
UNRAVELING THE TRUTH

THE ADRIATIC SEA shimmered under the moonlight as the yacht came into view, its sleek silhouette cutting through the gentle waves. From a distance, it looked serene—an unassuming luxury vessel nestled among the quiet waters. But Jack Jones knew better. This was Isaac's command center, the nerve hub of a sprawling criminal network orchestrating chaos across Europe.

Jack adjusted the binoculars and passed them to Irina Stepanov, who crouched beside him on the speedboat. "Looks like he's throwing a party," he murmured.

Through the lenses, Irina saw figures moving on the deck, laughter and the clink of glasses carrying faintly over the water. Her focus sharpened as she spotted armed guards patrolling the perimeter.

"Party's just a cover," Irina replied, her voice low. "This is where he's coordinating the attacks. We stop this, we cripple him."

Jack adjusted his earpiece, but his focus was elsewhere, his jaw tightening as he considered the risks they'd taken to get here. Before he could voice his doubts, his radio crackled with static—a voice breaking through that froze him mid-breath.

"Jack," came Amy's voice, strained and trembling.

Jack's head snapped up. "Amy? How are you on this frequency? Where are you?"

"Jack, I—" Her words cut off abruptly, replaced by another voice. Isaac's voice.

"Agent Jones," Isaac drawled, calm and cold. "You've been such a thorn in my side. It's almost a shame to see this end. Almost."

Jack's hand clenched into a fist. "What have you done?"

"Your sister is safe. For now," Isaac said. "But her safety depends entirely on your choices. Leave my operation intact, walk away, and she lives. Try to stop me, and you'll never see her again."

Irina grabbed Jack's arm, her voice low but forceful. "He's bluffing. He's trying to rattle you."

"You think I'd bluff about family, Stepanov?" Isaac's tone was mocking. "Let's test that theory."

The line went dead. Jack's pulse thundered as he looked at Irina, his face a mask of barely controlled rage.

"We have to end this now," Irina said sharply. "If we hesitate, he wins."

Jack hesitated, the weight of Isaac's threat bearing down on him. Finally, he nodded, his voice cold. "We end him. No matter the cost."

THE SPEEDBOAT GLIDED SILENTLY toward the yacht, its engine cut to avoid detection. Jack and Irina slipped into the water, their wetsuits blending with the dark waves. The cold bit into Jack's skin as they swam to the yacht's underside, where a maintenance hatch offered their best point of entry.

Irina reached the hatch first, pulling out a compact toolkit. The sea was eerily calm, the lapping waves masking the tension building between them.

"Make it quick," Jack muttered, keeping his eyes on the shadows above.

"Don't rush me," Irina snapped, her fingers working with practiced efficiency.

Moments later, the lock clicked open. Irina slipped inside first, her movements silent and deliberate. Jack followed, his senses on high alert.

The narrow corridors of the yacht were dimly lit, the hum of the engines vibrating through the walls. Jack pulled his pistol, gesturing for Irina to lead. "Where to?"

Irina consulted a schematic on her wrist tablet. "The bridge is two levels up. That's where we'll find Isaac—or whoever's pulling the strings tonight."

THE CLIMB through the yacht was slow and deliberate, each step calculated to avoid detection. They passed through a storage room filled with crates stamped with Cyrillic lettering, confirming Dimitri's intel about arms shipments. Jack took a mental note of the inventory as they moved on.

The sound of muffled voices guided them toward a doorway leading to the main deck. Irina held up a hand, signaling Jack to stop as she peeked through the crack.

"Four guards," she murmured. "All armed."

Jack grinned faintly. "Piece of cake."

Irina shot him a look but didn't argue. Instead, she pulled a flash grenade from her belt, arming it with a click. The grenade rolled into the room, detonating in a blinding flash. Shouts of confusion followed.

Jack and Irina moved as one. Jack disarmed the first guard with a swift blow to the temple, while Irina took out the second with a calculated strike to the throat. Within moments, all four guards were down, the room falling silent.

"Efficient," Jack said, catching his breath.

"Don't get comfortable," Irina replied, already moving toward a stairwell. "We're not done."

THE BRIDGE WAS BATHED in soft blue light, the hum of control panels underscoring the calm precision of Isaac's operative. The man stood at the center, issuing commands into a headset. "Phase one begins at dawn. Confirm readiness."

Irina stepped into the room, her pistol aimed. "Rethink that plan."

The operative turned slowly, his smirk unnerving. "Agent Stepanov. Agent Jones. Right on schedule."

Jack flanked her, his pistol raised. "You're going to shut it all down. Now."

The man chuckled, gesturing to the screens behind him. Live feeds showed protests, explosions, and riots unfolding across multiple cities. "This is just the beginning," he said. "Even if you kill me, you can't stop it."

"Where's Isaac?" Irina demanded.

The operative's smirk widened. "Closer than you think."

Before either could react, the door behind them slammed shut with a hiss. Isaac's voice crackled through the intercom.

"Welcome to my stage," Isaac said, his tone almost amused. "Did you really think I wouldn't prepare for this moment? You've walked into my trap, and now you'll die in it."

A countdown appeared on the screens, seconds ticking away. Irina rushed to the control panel, her fingers flying over the keyboard.

"We can't let this go off," she muttered.

"What's the play?" Jack asked, covering the door as footsteps echoed down the corridor.

"Override the system. But it'll take time." Her voice was steady, but Jack could see the strain in her movements.

He turned back toward the operative, his pistol aimed. "How do we stop it?"

The man's smirk didn't falter. "You don't."

Jack's grip tightened, his jaw clenching. "Then you're coming with us."

THE COUNTDOWN FROZE with less than thirty seconds remaining. Irina exhaled sharply, her shoulders sagging as the tension broke. "Got it."

The yacht shuddered as alarms blared, Isaac's operatives realizing the breach. Jack grabbed Irina's arm. "Time to move."

They retraced their steps, dodging guards as the pursuit intensified.

At the maintenance hatch, Jack covered their escape, his pistol snapping off shots as Irina slipped into the water.

They hit the sea just as bullets peppered the surface around them. Jack hauled himself onto the waiting speedboat, pulling Irina aboard as the driver gunned the engine.

THE BOAT SPED toward the horizon, the yacht shrinking into the distance. Jack pulled the tablet from his pack, scanning the data Irina had decrypted. It wasn't just attack plans—it was Isaac's entire network, from financial backers to covert operatives.

"This could dismantle everything," Jack said, awe in his voice.

Irina nodded, her expression guarded. "Or it could paint targets on our backs."

Jack leaned back, the weight of the tablet heavy in his lap. "You ever think about what happens after this?" he asked quietly.

Irina's gaze remained on the horizon. "After Isaac? After the missions?"

Jack nodded.

"There's no after, Jones," she said softly. "Not for people like us."

The silence stretched between them, broken only by the hum of the engine. Finally, Jack spoke, his voice firm. "Then let's make this one count."

CHAPTER 10
THE GAME CHANGES

THE SMALL VILLAGE in the Italian countryside was a stark contrast to the chaos Jack Jones and Irina Stepanov had left behind on the Adriatic. Red-tiled rooftops dotted the landscape, nestled among vineyards and olive groves that stretched for miles under a golden sunrise. But for Jack and Irina, this was no sanctuary—only a fleeting reprieve.

Inside the safe house, Irina paced the room, the faint light casting shadows across her tense features. On the table before her, the tablet recovered from Isaac's yacht hummed softly, its screen filled with lines of decrypted data. Each line told a story of corruption, betrayal, and a criminal empire that reached further than either of them had imagined.

Jack leaned against the wall, arms crossed, watching her with a mix of admiration and unease. "You've been staring at that thing for hours. Any breakthroughs?"

Irina stopped pacing but didn't look at him. "Isaac's network isn't just global. It's embedded in places we never expected—political offices, intelligence agencies... even humanitarian organizations."

Jack straightened, his jaw tightening. "You're saying there's no clear way to dismantle it?"

She finally met his gaze, her green eyes sharp. "I'm saying taking

Isaac down might only be the beginning. Too many players have a vested interest in keeping this web intact."

Jack exhaled, running a hand through his hair. "Farrow's going to love that."

Irina's lips twitched, but it wasn't a smile. "If he gets this intel. We haven't decided where it goes yet."

THE SOUND of an approaching vehicle shattered the stillness. Jack moved to the window, peering through a gap in the curtains. A black SUV rumbled down the dirt road, dust billowing in its wake.

"We've got company," he said, grabbing his pistol. "Friendly or otherwise?"

Irina joined him, her expression hardening. "Given our track record, I'd bet on otherwise."

The SUV came to a stop outside the safe house, its engine idling. The doors opened, and three men in tactical gear stepped out, their movements precise and deliberate. Jack's stomach sank as he recognized the lead figure—Anton Karpov, the freelance operative they'd crossed paths with in Vienna.

"Karpov," Jack muttered. "Looks like he's still holding a grudge."

Irina moved to the table, quickly tucking the tablet into her pack. "We can't let them take the data."

Jack nodded, his grip tightening on his pistol. "Then we don't let them."

THE FIRST GUNSHOT shattered the quiet, followed by a barrage of fire that tore through the walls of the safe house. Jack and Irina ducked behind cover, returning fire as the air filled with the acrid smell of gunpowder.

"They're trying to flush us out," Jack said, reloading his weapon. "What's the plan?"

Irina's gaze darted to the pack slung over her shoulder. "We split up. You draw them away, and I get the data out of here."

Jack hesitated, his instincts screaming against the idea. "You're kidding. If they catch you—"

"They won't," she cut him off, her voice firm. "But if we stay together, neither of us gets out."

Jack's jaw tightened, but he knew she was right. "Fine. But if this goes sideways—"

"It won't," she said, her tone softer now. "Just... don't do anything stupid."

Jack smirked, his tension easing slightly. "Who, me?"

Irina's faint smile vanished as she tossed him a smoke grenade. "Go. I'll cover you."

THE SMOKE GRENADE DETONATED, filling the room with a thick, choking cloud. Jack moved first, slipping out the back door as gunfire continued. Irina stayed behind, her shots precise as she kept Karpov's men pinned down.

Outside, Jack sprinted through the vineyard, his footsteps muffled by the soft earth. The SUV roared to life behind him, its headlights cutting through the early morning mist as it gave chase.

"Come on," Jack muttered, weaving between the rows of vines. He fired a few shots over his shoulder, hitting one of the tires and sending the vehicle skidding off course.

Back at the safe house, Irina moved swiftly, her every motion calculated. She took down the last of Karpov's men with a single, clean shot before slipping out through a hidden exit. The tablet was secure, but the danger was far from over.

JACK AND IRINA reconvened at a predetermined rendezvous point—a crumbling stone chapel on the outskirts of the village. Jack was already there, leaning against the altar and catching his breath when Irina arrived.

"Miss me?" he asked, his smirk widening as she glared at him.

"You're lucky you're still alive," she shot back, though there was no venom in her tone.

Jack's expression sobered as he motioned to the tablet. "What's the move? Do we hand it over to EISA or NESA?"

Irina hesitated, her gaze locked on the device. "Neither."

Jack raised an eyebrow. "You've got another plan?"

She nodded. "This data isn't just a tool to stop Isaac. It's a weapon —one that could destroy trust in every institution it touches. If we give it to the wrong hands..."

"It's chaos," Jack finished, his tone grim. "So what do we do?"

Irina's lips curved into a faint, almost sad smile. "We go rogue. Release it ourselves—selectively. Make sure it ends up where it can do the most good."

Jack chuckled, shaking his head. "You really know how to complicate things, Stepanov."

"Coming from you?" she replied, arching an eyebrow. "I'll take that as a compliment."

As the first rays of sunlight filtered through the chapel's broken windows, Jack and Irina prepared to move. Their partnership was far from perfect, but in that moment, they understood each other completely.

"This isn't over," Jack said, slipping the tablet into his jacket.

Irina met his gaze, her expression unreadable. "It never is."

They stepped out into the dawn, the weight of the mission—and the war still ahead—settling over them. Isaac's network was wounded, but not defeated. And as Jack and Irina disappeared into the horizon, they knew the hardest battles were yet to come.

The End

DOUBLE CROSSED

A SHORT THRILLER

CHAPTER 1
A TRAP IN BRUSSELS

THE EUROPEAN UNION'S headquarters in Brussels was a monument to power and diplomacy, its glass façade gleaming under a pale winter sun. Inside, the energy was electric. Delegates from across Europe moved through the vast atrium, their tailored suits and sharp heels clicking against polished marble floors. Conversations ranged from global security to corporate deals, but beneath the polished surface lurked a web of private agendas and hidden alliances.

Jack Jones scanned the crowd, his casual demeanor masking the focus in his sharp blue eyes. Every detail mattered—the way a nervous aide fidgeted with their tie, the sudden quiet around a private conversation, the presence of security teams that didn't quite match the EU's standard protocol.

Adjusting his tie, Jack muttered into his concealed mic, "You sure this is the place? Looks like a very expensive cocktail hour to me."

Irina Stepanov's voice came through his earpiece, calm and precise. "Herrick is here. Elevator B. Heading to the tenth floor."

Jack's lips quirked into a faint smile. "And here I thought you were just making me wear a suit for fun."

Across the room, Irina sipped from a champagne flute, her green eyes scanning the crowd over the rim. Dressed in a dark emerald blouse and pencil skirt, she blended seamlessly into the high-society environment. The air of elegance disguised her razor-sharp focus—and the small knife strapped to her thigh.

"I make you wear a suit because you're easier to spot otherwise," Irina replied. "Now stop talking and move."

Jack glanced toward the elevators just as the polished doors of Elevator B slid shut, Markus Herrick's tall figure disappearing inside. Jack didn't need to look twice to confirm—the silver-haired logistics expert matched the photo in his briefing. Herrick wasn't just one of Isaac Fontaine's trusted lieutenants; he was the man who made Isaac's empire run like clockwork.

"Think he knows we're here?" Jack asked as he strode across the atrium.

Irina's voice was flat. "If he doesn't, he's about to."

THE ELEVATOR CARRIED Jack to the tenth floor, its mirrored walls reflecting his composed expression. His fingers brushed the concealed holster under his jacket, a reminder of just how quickly things could go sideways.

When the doors opened, Jack stepped into a long corridor lined with frosted-glass conference rooms. Soft voices and the hum of air conditioning filled the space. At the far end of the hall, Herrick and his two bodyguards stood outside a corner room. Herrick glanced at his watch, his posture relaxed but his eyes sharp.

"Target is stationary," Jack murmured. "Irina, what's your status?"

"Two floors below. Planting a secondary transmitter near the server room," she replied. "Give me two minutes."

"Take your time," Jack muttered. "I'll just be here, casually eaves-dropping on Europe's most wanted logistics manager."

Leaning casually against the wall, Jack pulled out his phone, pretending to scroll through emails while his attention remained fixed on Herrick. One of the bodyguards glanced his way, and Jack offered a polite, disinterested nod. The man's gaze lingered before returning to Herrick.

Jack felt the hairs on the back of his neck prickle. Something about this didn't feel right—the bodyguards' attention was too focused, their movements too deliberate.

"Irina," he said quietly. "This might be more complicated than we thought."

DOWNSTAIRS, Irina worked quickly, her focus unwavering as she affixed a small transmitter beneath the server rack. The server room hummed with energy, its rows of blinking lights casting eerie shadows across the walls.

"Bug planted," she murmured into her mic. "Signal is live."

"Good timing," Jack said. "Because I think we're about to have company."

The sound of elevator doors opening behind him confirmed it. Jack glanced over his shoulder and saw four men in tactical gear stepping into the hallway. They moved with precision, their uniforms bearing a private security insignia Jack didn't recognize.

"Definitely company," Jack muttered, straightening.

The lead bodyguard at Herrick's side said something quietly, and Herrick's head snapped toward Jack. His expression darkened.

Irina's voice came through Jack's earpiece, sharp and urgent. "Get out of there now. That's not local security—they're private contractors. Armed."

Jack was already moving.

THE FIRST SHOT shattered the relative quiet of the hallway, sending employees diving for cover behind conference room doors. Jack ducked into a nearby alcove, drawing his pistol and returning fire.

At the other end of the hall, Herrick slipped into the corner conference room, flanked by his bodyguards. The tactical team advanced, their weapons raised as they methodically swept the area.

"Jack, where are you?" Irina's voice was clipped.

"Top floor," Jack replied, firing twice to pin down the advancing team. "Your friends brought backup."

"I told you to stay subtle," Irina snapped.

Jack grinned despite himself. "Subtle is overrated."

IRINA MOVED SWIFTLY through the atrium, her heels clicking against the marble floor. The sound of gunfire had sent most of the attendees scattering for the exits, but Irina barely noticed them. Her focus was on the staircase that led to the tenth floor.

She reached the top just as Jack dove through the doorway of a side office, rolling to his feet with his pistol drawn.

"Having fun?" Irina asked dryly.

Jack's response was cut off by another burst of gunfire. Irina returned fire, forcing the tactical team to take cover.

"We're not getting out the way we came in," she said.

Jack's gaze darted around the office. His eyes landed on a ventilation shaft above the filing cabinets. "Ventilation?"

Irina raised an eyebrow. "This is your brilliant plan?"

"Unless you have a better one," Jack shot back, already climbing onto the desk.

Irina sighed, holstering her weapon as she followed him into the narrow metal tunnel.

THE VENTILATION SHAFT was cramped and stifling, but it offered a clear path to the service corridor near the rear of the building. Jack dropped down first, his weapon ready as he scanned the dimly lit space.

"All clear," he said, helping Irina down.

They slipped out into the alley, the sound of distant sirens growing louder. Jack gestured toward a delivery truck idling near the loading dock. "Think they'll give us a lift?"

Irina didn't reply, her attention focused on her phone. The transmitter she'd planted upstairs was already transmitting Herrick's signal.

"He's moving," she said. "Berlin."

Jack raised an eyebrow. "Looks like our work here isn't done."

"No," Irina agreed, a faint smile tugging at her lips. "It's just beginning."

CHAPTER 2
SAFE HOUSE SECRETS

THE SAFE HOUSE was buried deep in Berlin's industrial outskirts, a nondescript warehouse surrounded by rusted shipping containers and graffiti-streaked walls. Inside, the air was stale, tinged with the faint metallic tang of oil and dust. A folding table in the center of the room was piled with equipment: a laptop, communication devices, and a tangled mess of surveillance gear.

Jack dropped his duffel bag onto the floor with a heavy thud, scanning the room with a grimace. "Charming place you've got here."

Irina didn't respond, already unzipping her bag to pull out a portable server. Her focus was sharp, her movements methodical as she connected it to the laptop.

"I'm guessing this isn't an EISA-approved property," Jack continued, leaning against the wall with a faint smirk.

"It's not," Irina replied curtly. "That's why it's still standing."

Jack chuckled softly but let the comment slide. He moved toward the window, peeling back a sliver of the heavy blackout curtains to watch the empty street outside. "So, what do we have on Herrick?"

"Give me a moment," Irina said, her fingers flying across the keyboard. The laptop screen filled with lines of code as she accessed the transmitter she'd planted. "The signal's clean. He stopped moving an hour ago, somewhere near Friedrichstraße."

Jack turned from the window, frowning. "Friedrichstraße? That's high-profile territory for a logistics guy."

Irina nodded. "It gets better. I pulled metadata from the files he uploaded during the conference. Guess whose credentials were used to access them?"

"Isaac's?" Jack guessed.

Irina shook her head. "Maria Ortega."

Jack's expression darkened. "Your boss."

"Yes," Irina replied, her voice tight. "And there's more. Those files? They were flagged as restricted by EISA's internal systems. Ortega shouldn't have had access unless someone higher up gave it to her."

Jack crossed his arms, watching her carefully. "What are you saying? That EISA's working with Isaac?"

"I'm saying that either Ortega is freelancing, or EISA is using me to clean up something they don't want exposed." Irina's green eyes met Jack's, her expression hard. "Either way, we can't trust them."

Jack snorted softly. "Welcome to the club."

THE TENSION between them lingered as Irina pulled up a map of Friedrichstraße, highlighting a sleek office building nestled among high-end boutiques and cafés. "This is where Herrick's signal is coming from," she said. "It's listed as a private consulting firm, but it's likely a front."

Jack leaned over her shoulder, studying the map. "High foot traffic, lots of surveillance. It'll be tough to get in without making noise."

"We don't need to go in," Irina said. "If Herrick's there, he's meeting someone important. We monitor him from a distance, intercept any communications, and leave no trace."

Jack raised an eyebrow. "Since when are you a fan of the quiet approach?"

"I'm a fan of surviving," Irina shot back.

The two worked in silence for the next hour, setting up surveillance equipment and synchronizing their communication systems. Jack's movements were steady but distracted, his thoughts clearly elsewhere.

"Spit it out," Irina said finally, not looking up from her laptop.

Jack hesitated. "Your boss. Ortega. How deep do you think she's in?"

Irina sighed, leaning back in her chair. "I don't know. She's been in EISA for twenty years, and she's built her reputation on results. But lately... things haven't added up."

"Like her ordering you to arrest me in Munich?" Jack asked, his tone sharper than he intended.

Irina flinched slightly but didn't rise to the bait. "Exactly like that."

Jack exhaled, his frustration palpable. "Look, I get it. Questioning your own agency—it's not easy. But if EISA's playing both sides, we need to know."

"And if NESA is using you as bait to draw out Isaac?" Irina countered.

Jack didn't answer immediately. Instead, he turned back to the window, his jaw tight. "Maybe we're both expendable."

Irina's voice softened. "We're not."

LATER THAT NIGHT, the surveillance feed from Friedrichstraße flickered to life. Herrick's unmistakable figure appeared, stepping out of a sleek black sedan and striding into the building's lobby. A second figure emerged from the car, their face obscured by a hood.

"Who's that?" Jack asked, leaning closer.

"Not sure yet," Irina replied, enhancing the feed. The figure moved with deliberate precision, their posture confident but unassuming. "Could be one of Isaac's operatives. Or someone higher up."

"Great," Jack muttered. "A mystery guest."

The feed shifted as Herrick and the hooded figure entered a private conference room on the second floor. Irina switched to an external audio device, her fingers adjusting the frequency.

"Anything?" Jack asked.

"Static," Irina replied. "The room's shielded. They're expecting trouble."

"Then we give them trouble," Jack said, already moving toward his gear.

"Not yet," Irina warned, her tone firm. "We don't have enough intel. If we go in blind, we could lose more than we gain."

Jack hesitated, then nodded reluctantly. "Fine. But we stay close. If Herrick moves, we follow."

Irina's lips curved into a faint smile. "For once, we agree."

HOURS LATER, as dawn began to break over Berlin, Irina's laptop beeped. The encrypted file she'd been analyzing had finally decrypted, revealing a series of coordinates and timestamps.

Jack leaned over her shoulder, frowning. "What am I looking at?"

"Shipping manifests," Irina replied. "Linked to Isaac's operations. Arms, explosives, even biochemicals. And they're moving fast."

Jack's stomach tightened. "Where's the next shipment?"

Irina's expression darkened. "Paris. And we're already behind schedule."

CHAPTER 3
PARISIAN SHADOWS

THE LOUVRE at night was a vision of timeless beauty and quiet menace. Under the glow of the moon, its glass pyramid sparkled like a beacon against the darkened Paris skyline. Inside, the charity gala hosted by one of Europe's most influential foundations provided the perfect cover for clandestine deals and veiled threats.

Jack Jones adjusted the cuffs of his tuxedo as he stepped out of the hired car, scanning the well-dressed crowd filtering through the entrance. Security guards in sharp black suits were stationed at intervals, their earpieces glinting under the soft lights. Jack's smirk was faint but confident as he offered an arm to Irina Stepanov, who emerged beside him in an elegant navy gown that flowed like liquid silk.

"You look stunning," he murmured.

Irina didn't break stride. "Don't let it distract you."

Jack chuckled. "Distracted? Me? Never."

But his grin faded as his gaze shifted to the ornate entrance. Somewhere inside, Markus Herrick was set to meet with an operative tied to *The Veil*. Their mission was clear: intercept the intel, identify the players, and get out without drawing attention.

"Remember the plan," Irina said, her voice low as they approached the security checkpoint.

"Blend in, gather intel, don't die," Jack replied. "Got it."

INSIDE THE LOUVRE'S grand hall, the atmosphere was thick with opulence and concealed agendas. Crystal chandeliers cast a warm glow over the marble floors, while murmurs of conversation rose and fell like waves. Waiters weaved through the crowd, carrying trays of champagne and hors d'oeuvres.

Jack moved through the room with the ease of someone who belonged, mingling with diplomats and business elites while keeping his attention on Herrick. The silver-haired operative stood near a sculpture display, speaking in hushed tones with a man in a tailored gray suit.

"Gray suit," Jack murmured into his lapel mic. "That's the guy?"

Irina's voice came through his earpiece, calm and clipped. "Confirmed. Pierre Gautier, former intelligence operative turned corporate consultant. Rumored ties to *The Veil's* financial operations."

Jack's smile didn't waver as he accepted a glass of champagne from a passing waiter. "Think he'll spill his secrets over a drink?"

"Unlikely," Irina replied. "Stay close. I'll move in from the other side."

Irina circled the room, her movements calculated and deliberate. She exchanged pleasantries with a French ambassador and a technology CEO, using the interactions as cover to position herself closer to Herrick and Gautier. Her clutch concealed a discreet recording device, ready to capture their conversation once she was within range.

But as she moved, a familiar voice stopped her cold.

"Irina Stepanov," Maria Ortega said, stepping into view with a practiced smile. "It's been too long."

Irina's pulse quickened, but her expression remained neutral. "Maria. I didn't expect to see you here."

Maria, dressed in a sleek black dress, tilted her head slightly. "Oh, I imagine there's quite a bit you didn't expect. Shall we talk?"

Jack's earpiece crackled with static, followed by Irina's voice. "Change of plans. Ortega's here."

Jack frowned, his grip tightening on the champagne flute. "What? Why?"

"Unclear," Irina replied. "She just pulled me aside."

"Watch yourself," Jack muttered, scanning the room for signs of trouble.

IN A QUIET ALCOVE near the edge of the hall, Maria's expression hardened, her smile fading. "You've been busy, Irina. Munich. Rome. Brussels. Your movements haven't exactly gone unnoticed."

Irina crossed her arms, her tone steady. "I'm doing my job."

"Are you?" Maria asked, her voice lowering. "Because from where I stand, it looks like you're working against us."

Irina's jaw tightened. "Us?"

Maria leaned in, her tone cold. "EISA isn't blind, Irina. You're walking a very fine line. And Jack Jones? He's not your ally. He's a liability."

Irina didn't flinch. "What are you suggesting?"

"Arrest him," Maria said flatly. "Bring him in, and we can resolve this cleanly. Refuse, and you'll leave me no choice but to act."

ACROSS THE ROOM, Jack continued his surveillance. Herrick and Gautier were deep in conversation, their faces grim. Jack adjusted his position, angling closer without drawing attention.

He didn't notice the man approaching until it was too late.

"Jack Jones," a smooth voice said behind him.

Jack turned, his body tensing. The man before him was impeccably dressed, with an air of authority that set him apart from the other guests.

"Do I know you?" Jack asked, his tone light but wary.

The man smiled faintly. "No, but I know you. And I have a message for you: Stay out of EISA's way."

Jack's smile thinned. "EISA? What's their interest in me?"

The man's gaze was cold. "Let's just say your presence complicates things. If you're smart, you'll walk away before you find yourself in over your head."

THE TENSION in the room was palpable as Jack and Irina reconnected near the central display.

"Ortega wants you arrested," Irina said quietly, her tone grim.

"And your friends are telling me to back off," Jack replied. "Looks like everyone here is playing their own game."

Irina's expression was unreadable, but her green eyes burned with intensity. "We need to leave. Now."

Jack glanced toward Herrick and Gautier. "We don't have the intel yet."

"Then we improvise," Irina said, already moving toward the exit.

THEIR ESCAPE WAS chaotic but controlled. Irina activated the recording device in her clutch, capturing snippets of Herrick's conversation as they moved. Jack deflected the attention of a security guard with a well-timed distraction, allowing them to slip into a side corridor.

By the time they reached the car waiting outside, Jack's mind was racing.

"What did Ortega say to you?" he asked as the car pulled away.

Irina hesitated. "She gave me a choice. Turn you in or face the consequences."

Jack's jaw tightened. "And what did you tell her?"

"I told her nothing," Irina replied, meeting his gaze. "But this isn't over."

Jack nodded, his expression grim. "No, it's not."

As the lights of Paris faded behind them, Jack and Irina both knew the mission had just become far more dangerous—and far more personal.

CHAPTER 4
TENSIONS IN THE ALPS

THE MOUNTAIN AIR was sharp and cold, biting at Jack's face as he stepped out of the rented Jeep. The remote cabin lay nestled in a snow-dusted clearing, surrounded by towering pines and jagged peaks that seemed to touch the sky. It was the kind of place where secrets stayed buried—or where people went to disappear.

Jack pulled his jacket tighter against the chill, his breath forming clouds in the crisp air. "Nice and secluded," he muttered, surveying the area. "I'm guessing this isn't on Airbnb."

Irina Stepanov stepped out from the passenger side, her scarf pulled high against the biting wind. She scanned the clearing with the practiced efficiency of someone who'd learned not to trust silence. "No movement. Looks secure."

Jack glanced at her, a faint smirk tugging at his lips. "I'll take your word for it."

The tension between them had been simmering since Paris. Maria Ortega's ultimatum and the shadowy warning Jack had received had left cracks in their partnership. Trust was fragile, and here in the Alps, surrounded by isolation and danger, it felt even thinner.

THE CABIN WAS small but functional. A wood-burning stove stood in one corner, its faint warmth doing little to offset the icy draft seeping through the walls. A heavy wooden table dominated the center of the room, its surface scarred by years of use.

Jack set his bag on the table, unzipping it to reveal an array of gear: weapons, surveillance equipment, and a portable server. "Not exactly cozy, but it'll do."

Irina moved toward a hidden panel in the wall, pressing it open to reveal a locked compartment. From inside, she retrieved a laptop and several folders. Her expression was unreadable. "We're not here to relax."

"Could've fooled me," Jack said, brushing off a chair before sitting down. "What's in the files?"

Irina opened one of the folders, spreading the documents across the table. "Shipping manifests, encrypted communications, and payment records tied to Isaac's operations. These are direct links to his network."

Jack leaned forward, studying the papers. The manifests listed arms shipments, explosives, and biochemicals, with destinations across Europe. His stomach tightened as he realized the scale of Isaac's plans.

"This isn't just about money," Jack said, his voice grim. "He's gearing up for something big."

Irina nodded, her tone hard. "Coordinated attacks. Multiple targets across Europe. These shipments are the puzzle pieces. We need to figure out where and when they'll strike."

HOURS PASSED as they sifted through the intel, their focus interrupted only by the occasional crackle of the wood stove. Jack's usual banter was absent, replaced by a quiet intensity as he worked.

Leaning back in his chair, Jack stared at the papers in front of him. The words blurred, replaced by memories he couldn't suppress—the screams in Munich, the sound of collapsing walls, and Amy's voice on the phone after he'd made it home.

"Jack," Irina's voice broke through his thoughts. She was watching him, her expression sharp.

He forced a faint smirk. "What's on your mind, Stepanov? Another clever plan to keep me out of trouble?"

Irina didn't answer immediately, her green eyes narrowing. "You've been staring at that page for ten minutes. Either you've found something critical, or you're thinking about something else entirely."

Jack sighed, running a hand through his hair. "Munich."

Irina's gaze softened, just barely. "The op?"

Jack nodded. "It should've gone differently. We were supposed to save lives, but I watched everything fall apart. Amy's never said it, but I know she blames me for the silence afterward, for the distance. Maybe she's right."

Irina studied him for a moment before speaking. "If guilt were enough to stop you, you wouldn't be here. Use it—but don't let it control you."

Her tone was steady, but her words carried an edge of something Jack couldn't place—understanding, or perhaps warning.

IRINA TAPPED one of the documents, drawing Jack's attention back to the table. "There's a pattern here. The shipments are timed to arrive in Paris, Berlin, and Rome on the same day. That's no coincidence."

Jack frowned, leaning closer. "Coordinated chaos. Hit major cities at the same time—overwhelm the response. Classic Fontaine."

Irina nodded. "And The Veil. They're funding this, using Isaac as the executor."

Jack exhaled slowly, leaning back in his chair. "We're going to need more than this to stop it. What else is in that hidden panel of yours?"

Irina hesitated, her gaze shifting to the compartment.

"Something you're not telling me?" Jack asked, his tone sharper now.

Irina's jaw tightened. "I have my orders, Jack."

"Orders," Jack said, taking a step back, his voice low but sharp. "Is that all this is to you? Following the script, no matter the cost?"

Irina's eyes flashed, a rare crack in her composure. "And what about you? How do I know your people aren't playing you the same way? Maybe NESA doesn't care about the fallout—just the headlines."

Jack shook his head, his tone bitter. "You really think I don't ask myself that every day? The difference is, I make my choices. You're still waiting for someone to tell you what yours are."

The words landed hard, and for a moment, Irina didn't respond. Then she straightened, her voice cold. "We don't have time for this."

"Make time," Jack pressed. "If we're going into Zurich together, I need to know you've got my back. Not EISA's."

Irina's gaze was steady, but something flickered in her expression— doubt, or perhaps something deeper. "If I didn't, we wouldn't be standing here."

THE CRUNCH of snow outside shattered the tension. Both operatives froze, their hands instinctively going to their weapons. Jack moved to the window, peering out into the darkness.

"Movement," he murmured. "Two figures, maybe more. Armed."

Irina grabbed her pistol, her voice low but steady. "They've found us."

Jack's lips curved into a grim smile. "Guess we're not as secluded as we thought."

THE FIRST GUNSHOT shattered the quiet, splintering the wooden frame of the window. Jack dove for cover, firing back toward the treeline. The cabin erupted into chaos as more shots rang out, the attackers advancing in coordinated waves.

"Side door!" Irina shouted, firing through the broken window. "They're flanking us!"

Jack grabbed a flashbang from his bag, tossing it toward the door just as it burst open. The explosion of light and sound sent the attackers reeling, buying them precious seconds to regroup.

"We can't hold this position," Irina said, her voice tight.

"Not planning to," Jack replied, pulling her toward the rear of the cabin. "There's a back exit. Go!"

They sprinted into the snowy forest, the cold biting at their faces as bullets tore through the trees around them. Jack led the way, his mind racing as he calculated their next move.

BY THE TIME they reached the cover of a rocky outcrop, the gunfire had faded into the distance. Jack leaned against the cold stone, catching his breath.

Irina crouched beside him, her weapon still drawn. "They knew we were here. Someone tipped them off."

Jack nodded, his expression grim. "And they're not giving up anytime soon."

Irina's gaze was distant, her mind already calculating their next steps. "We need to keep moving. If they have our location, the cabin's compromised. We can't stay in one place for long."

Jack glanced at her, his tone softening. "Still with me?"

Irina blinked, snapping back to the present. "Always."

Jack nodded, his resolve hardening. "Good. Because this isn't over."

CHAPTER 5
CAT-AND-MOUSE IN ISTANBUL

THE NARROW STREETS of Istanbul were alive with chaos and energy. The city's vibrant markets, neon signs, and the haunting call to prayer created a symphony that enveloped Jack Jones as he moved through the crowd. Somewhere in this maze, Markus Herrick was meeting with a Veil emissary—a shadowy figure who might hold the key to Isaac Fontaine's next move.

Jack adjusted his leather jacket, blending into the crowd of tourists and locals. The low hum of voices and the sharp scent of spices from the bazaar filled the air, but his focus was on the earpiece crackling in his ear.

"West side of the market," Irina Stepanov's voice came through, calm but clipped. "Two targets. Herrick and an unknown. I'll cover the exit."

Jack smirked, his tone light. "That's what I like about you, Irina—always the optimist."

"Just don't get yourself killed," she shot back.

Jack's smirk faded as he caught sight of Herrick's silver hair near a jewelry stall. The operative was speaking with a man in a crisp gray suit, his face partially obscured by the shadows of the alley. Jack slowed his pace, weaving between vendors and customers, positioning himself just close enough to hear snippets of their conversation.

"… shipments confirmed… no deviations…" Herrick's voice was low and deliberate.

The man in the suit nodded, his voice barely audible. "The network is secure. Fontaine expects results. Delays will not be tolerated."

JACK SLIPPED INTO THE SHADOWS, pulling a small parabolic microphone from his pocket. He adjusted the device, amplifying the conversation as he lingered near a spice stall.

"Istanbul is stable," Herrick said. "But the next phase requires discretion."

The man in the suit gave a thin smile. "Discretion is not a problem, provided your security holds."

Jack's grip tightened on the microphone. This was bigger than he'd anticipated. The mention of Istanbul as a staging ground meant Isaac's operations weren't limited to arms shipments—they were orchestrating something far more coordinated.

He tapped his earpiece. "Irina, I'm going to tail Herrick. He's moving east toward the docks."

"Wait," Irina replied sharply. "You're exposed. Fall back and regroup."

Jack ignored her, slipping through the crowd as Herrick and the Veil operative began to move.

THE ALLEYWAYS near the docks were quieter, their shadows deepened by flickering streetlights. Jack kept his distance, staying just close enough to follow the pair without drawing attention.

But he wasn't the only one watching.

A faint rustle behind him set Jack on edge. He spun, catching a glimpse of a tall, lean figure slipping into the shadows.

"Karpov," Jack muttered under his breath.

Irina's voice came through immediately. "What did you say?"

"Karpov's here," Jack said, his tone grim. "He's tailing me."

"Get out of there," Irina said urgently. "Karpov's not just a tracker —he's a closer."

Jack exhaled, his adrenaline spiking. He turned back to the alley just in time to see Herrick and the Veil operative disappear through a side door.

"This isn't over," Jack muttered, slipping into the shadows.

INSIDE THE DIMLY LIT BUILDING, Jack crouched behind a stack of crates, his pistol drawn. The room was cavernous, filled with shipping containers and industrial equipment. Herrick and the Veil operative stood near a metal table, where a laptop displayed a live map of Europe.

Jack strained to hear their conversation, but the sound of footsteps behind him shattered his concentration. He turned, his weapon raised, just as Karpov stepped into view.

The freelance operative's blue eyes gleamed in the dim light, his smile cold. "Jones. Always one step behind."

Jack didn't hesitate. He fired, but Karpov was faster, ducking behind a crate and returning fire. The noise echoed through the ware-house, drawing Herrick's attention.

"Move!" Herrick barked to the Veil operative.

THE FIGHT WAS fast and brutal. Karpov moved like a predator, his strikes precise and relentless. Jack countered with his own training, using the environment to his advantage. He ducked under a swinging pipe, slamming Karpov into a stack of crates before rolling clear of a knife strike.

"You're good," Karpov said, his voice almost admiring. "But not good enough."

"Guess we'll find out," Jack retorted, catching Karpov's wrist and twisting the knife free.

A sharp crack split the air as Irina appeared, her pistol aimed at

Karpov's shoulder. The shot forced him to retreat, his expression darkening as he disappeared into the shadows.

"You're welcome," Irina said as she approached.

Jack smirked, rubbing his shoulder. "And here I thought you didn't care."

"Let's go," Irina said curtly. "Herrick's gone, and we need to track him before he vanishes."

THE CHASE LED them to the docks, where a sleek speedboat was just pulling away from the pier. Herrick stood at the helm, his phone pressed to his ear as he disappeared into the night.

"Damn it," Jack muttered, lowering his weapon.

Irina scanned the area, her expression tight. "We're not done. Herrick left something behind."

She pointed to a discarded satchel near the water's edge. Inside, they found a flash drive and a dossier filled with encrypted files.

Jack's jaw tightened as he scanned the documents. "Coordinates. Shipment schedules. And one name—Fontaine."

Irina met his gaze, her green eyes burning with determination. "Then we keep moving."

Jack nodded, his smirk faint. "Next stop, the Adriatic."

CHAPTER 6
THE ADRIATIC PURSUIT

THE ADRIATIC SEA stretched endlessly under the moonlight, its surface calm and silver like a sheet of polished glass. In the distance, the sleek lines of a luxury yacht stood out against the dark horizon. An elegant, modern vessel, its exterior gleamed under the floodlights illuminating its decks—a floating stronghold hiding Isaac Fontaine's secrets.

Jack Jones crouched at the edge of a speedboat, the faint hum of its motor the only sound as he adjusted his binoculars. "Nice ride," he murmured, studying the guards patrolling the yacht's upper deck. "Think they'll let us aboard for the midnight buffet?"

Irina Stepanov knelt beside him, her pistol holstered but ready. Dressed in a black wetsuit, her red hair was tightly tied back, her sharp green eyes focused on the yacht. "If by buffet you mean an armed escort to the brig, sure."

Jack grinned. "Good thing we brought our RSVP." He tapped the waterproof case strapped to his chest, filled with explosives, transmitters, and encrypted drives for the intel they planned to steal.

Irina shot him a sidelong glance. "You're enjoying this too much."

Jack's grin widened. "And you're not?"

She didn't answer. Instead, she signaled to the driver to kill the motor. The speedboat slowed to a stop, drifting quietly in the shadow of the larger vessel.

"Ready?" she asked, pulling on her diving mask.

Jack slipped on his own mask and nodded. "Let's crash the party."

THE WATER WAS ICY, seeping through Jack's wetsuit as he swam toward the yacht. Each stroke felt like an eternity, the tension mounting with every pull. Above them, the faint sound of footsteps echoed as guards patrolled the deck.

Jack reached the yacht first, gripping the rope ladder dangling over the side. He waited until Irina joined him before climbing silently, each step deliberate to avoid detection.

They reached the lower deck, ducking behind a stack of crates. Jack scanned the area, his voice low through the comm link. "Two guards by the stairwell, another by the control panel. Armed but not alert."

"I'll take the control panel," Irina replied. "You handle the stairs."

Jack nodded, slipping into the shadows as Irina moved in the opposite direction.

THE GUARD at the control panel barely had time to react before Irina struck, her movements swift and silent. She grabbed his wrist, twisting the weapon free before delivering a precise blow to his temple. He crumpled without a sound, and she dragged his unconscious form behind the crates.

"Panel's clear," she whispered into her mic.

Jack was already at the stairwell, his silenced pistol raised. The first guard fell with a muted grunt, his partner following seconds later.

"Stairwell secure," Jack replied. "Moving to the next level."

THE YACHT'S interior was a study in luxury—polished wood paneling, plush carpets, and soft ambient lighting. Jack barely noticed the decor as he crept through the narrow hallways, his focus on the laptop tucked under his arm.

They reached the control room without incident, Irina quickly overriding the lock with a portable hacking device. Inside, screens displayed live feeds from the yacht's cameras, communication consoles, and a secured computer system.

"Start the upload," Irina said, placing a transmitter on the main console.

Jack plugged the flash drive into the computer, his fingers flying over the keyboard. "This should take about five minutes."

Irina moved to the window, scanning the decks. "We might not have five minutes. They'll notice the guards missing soon."

"Then let's make it quick," Jack replied, focusing on the screen.

THE DOWNLOAD WAS AT 80% when the first alarm blared.

"Of course," Jack muttered, pulling the drive from the console as Irina drew her weapon.

The sound of boots thundered down the hallway as guards converged on their position. Jack slapped a small explosive charge against the control panel.

"What are you doing?" Irina demanded.

"Leaving a goodbye note," Jack replied, grabbing her arm. "Time to go."

THE YACHT ERUPTED into chaos as the explosive detonated, plunging the control room into darkness and sending guards scrambling. Jack and Irina moved quickly, their steps silent amid the confusion.

They reached the lower deck just as Isaac Fontaine himself appeared at the top of the stairwell, his sharp suit untouched by the surrounding pandemonium.

"Leaving so soon?" Isaac called, his voice calm despite the blaring alarms.

Jack paused, his jaw tightening as their eyes met. "You've got bigger problems, Isaac."

Isaac's smile was faint but chilling. "Oh, I doubt that." He gestured to one of his guards. "Kill them."

BULLETS RICOCHETED off the walls as Jack and Irina dove behind cover. Jack returned fire, his shots precise, while Irina tossed a smoke grenade to obscure their escape.

"Move!" Jack shouted, leading the way to the outer deck.

The guards pursued relentlessly, but Jack and Irina reached the edge of the yacht and leapt into the cold Adriatic waters. The impact knocked the wind from Jack's lungs, but he pushed forward, his strokes steady as they swam toward the waiting speedboat.

BY THE TIME they climbed aboard, drenched and breathless, the yacht was a distant silhouette. Jack slumped onto the seat, his pulse racing as he pulled the laptop from his bag.

Irina sat beside him, wringing water from her hair. "What did we get?"

Jack opened the laptop, scanning the decrypted files. His face darkened as he read. "Coordinates. Names. Shipments. And..." He paused, turning the screen toward her.

Irina leaned closer, her jaw tightening. The final entry was a target list: high-profile locations across Europe, including Berlin, Paris, and Rome.

"This isn't just chaos," Jack said quietly. "This is war."

Irina's green eyes met his, her determination hardening. "Then we end it."

Jack nodded, the resolve in his voice matching hers. "Next stop, Rome."

CHAPTER 7
REFUGE IN ROME

THE VATICAN safe house was a sanctuary of secrets, tucked above an unassuming bookshop in the Trastevere district of Rome. From the outside, it looked like any other apartment on the cobblestone street, shutters drawn against the quiet rain falling on the city. But inside, the walls were reinforced, the windows bulletproof, and the bookshelves filled not just with old volumes but hidden compartments containing encrypted equipment and weaponry.

Jack Jones leaned back in a worn leather chair, his fingers drumming a restless rhythm on the armrest. The decryption progress bar on Irina Stepanov's laptop inched forward at an agonizing pace. The warm glow of the desk lamp did little to cut the tension that hung between them.

"How much longer?" Jack asked, breaking the silence.

Irina didn't look up from the screen, her tone flat. "Decryption doesn't speed up just because you complain about it."

Jack smirked faintly, though it didn't reach his eyes. "Worth a shot."

Irina's focus remained on the laptop as she adjusted the connection. "The files are big. And encrypted on a level that says Isaac didn't trust anyone with them—not even his own lieutenants."

Jack exhaled, his tone tinged with frustration. "We risked our necks for this intel. Let's hope it's worth it."

"It will be," Irina said firmly.

THE STOLEN files were a treasure trove of information—shipment manifests, coded orders, and logs of financial transactions that painted a damning picture of Isaac Fontaine's global network. But without the decryption key, the data was an infuriating maze of meaningless symbols.

Irina paused as one encrypted message caught her attention. Its header bore an unusual identifier: "Directive A."

Her eyes narrowed. "This one's different."

Jack moved to her side, leaning over her shoulder to study the file. "Directive A?"

Irina nodded, her expression darkening. "The Veil's inner council uses codenames. Directive A is one of their strategists—a top operative." She hesitated, her voice tightening. "I've crossed paths with them before."

Jack arched a brow. "And?"

"Munich," she said simply, the weight of the word hanging between them. "If Directive A is involved, this operation isn't just Isaac's. It's The Veil's."

Jack's jaw clenched. "You think they know you're here?"

Irina's green eyes met his. "If they do, they'll exploit it. We need to decode this and figure out Directive A's role. Fast."

THE HOURS STRETCHED on as they worked side by side, piecing together fragments of data and cross-referencing logs. The rain outside had stopped, leaving the room cloaked in a heavy silence broken only by the occasional clatter of keys.

Jack leaned back, rubbing the bridge of his nose. "What's the endgame for you, Irina? All this? The Veil? EISA?"

She didn't look up, her fingers still moving. "Stopping Isaac. Exposing The Veil. Making sure the people caught in their crossfire have a chance."

"And then?" Jack pressed. "What happens when there's no more mission to chase?"

Irina finally glanced at him, her expression unreadable. "For people like us, Jack? There's always another mission."

Jack leaned against the wall, his voice dropping. "What if there wasn't?"

Her lips twitched into a faint, almost bitter smile. "Then I guess we'd have to learn how to stop running."

THE DECRYPTION COMPLETED JUST after midnight, revealing a series of detailed plans, timelines, and target lists. The scope of Isaac's operation was staggering. Berlin, Paris, and Rome weren't just on the list—they were the keystones of a coordinated destabilization strategy.

"This isn't chaos," Irina murmured, her voice tight as she scrolled through the documents. "It's precision. If these plans succeed, Europe's infrastructure will collapse within days."

Jack's expression hardened. "This is war. And Directive A's pulling the strings."

Another file caught Irina's attention—an encrypted log marked "High-Level Operatives." She clicked it open, and her breath caught as the first name appeared.

"Maria Ortega," Jack read aloud, his voice grim.

Irina stared at the screen, her expression unreadable. "If she's this deep in, then EISA isn't just compromised—they're part of the operation."

Jack exhaled sharply, his frustration evident. "You've given years to this agency, Irina. Burned bridges, taken the hits. Don't tell me you're still willing to trust them."

Her gaze didn't waver. "I don't trust EISA. I trust the mission."

Before Jack could respond, the doorbell rang.

Jack's hand went to his weapon as Irina moved to the window, her movements precise and silent. She peered through the curtain, her tension easing only slightly.

"It's Dimitri."

Jack groaned. "Great. Just what we need—our favorite morally flexible arms dealer."

Dimitri Valenko stepped into the safe house, shedding his rain-slicked coat with practiced nonchalance. His sharp eyes swept the room, lingering on the laptop before landing on Jack and Irina.

"Well, well," Dimitri said with a smirk. "If it isn't Europe's most wanted. You've been busy, I hear."

"Cut the theatrics," Irina said curtly. "What do you know about Isaac's next move?"

Dimitri's smirk faded as he settled into a chair. "Isaac's doubling down. He knows you've disrupted his shipments, and he's preparing a counterstrike. But that's not his real play."

"Then what is?" Jack demanded.

Dimitri leaned forward, his tone serious. "Isaac's meeting with The Veil's financial backers in Vienna. That's where he's consolidating his power."

Irina's gaze narrowed. "If we can disrupt that meeting—"

"You can burn him," Dimitri finished. "But it won't be easy. Vienna's crawling with Veil operatives. And if Directive A's involved, they'll be ready for you."

Jack crossed his arms. "When are they not?"

As Dimitri left, the room fell silent. Jack leaned against the wall, watching as Irina packed her gear.

"Vienna's next," he said.

Irina nodded. "We take out Isaac's financial network, and we cripple his operation."

Jack smirked faintly. "High risk, low reward. Sounds like our kind of mission."

Irina allowed herself a small smile. "Let's get to work."

CHAPTER 8
THE VIENNA PLAY

THE VIENNA SKYLINE glowed under a crisp winter night, its historic architecture a stark backdrop to the modern shadows lurking within. The Imperial Hotel stood as a symbol of opulence and power, its grand façade illuminated by golden floodlights. Jack Jones adjusted his tie as he stepped out of the sleek black car, his eyes scanning the elegant crowds milling around the hotel's entrance.

"This is it," Jack murmured into his concealed mic. "Isaac's inside, and he's brought his financial backers to the party."

Irina Stepanov's voice came through his earpiece, calm and precise. "Stick to the plan. We infiltrate the meeting, extract the intel, and get out before anyone realizes we're here."

Jack smirked faintly as he joined the flow of dignitaries and elites heading toward the grand entrance. "Subtlety, huh? Not exactly our specialty."

"Maybe it should be," Irina quipped, her tone dry.

INSIDE, the Imperial Hotel was a testament to luxury: marble floors gleamed under crystal chandeliers, and the air carried the faint scent of polished wood and fresh flowers. Jack blended effortlessly into the sea of tuxedos and evening gowns, his practiced demeanor making him just another guest at a high-profile gala.

He caught sight of Irina across the room. Dressed in a sleek black evening gown that complemented her composed air, she moved with deliberate grace, her clutch concealing tools far more dangerous than cosmetics.

Her voice came through his earpiece. "Security's tight. Isaac's suite is on the twelfth floor, Room 1203. Two guards at the door, another two stationed in the hallway. Maria Ortega is in the building, but I can't confirm her location yet."

Jack exhaled, his smirk fading. "Complicates things. If she's involved, this isn't just about Isaac anymore."

"No," Irina agreed. "But it's our best shot at shutting both of them down."

THE ELEVATOR RIDE to the twelfth floor was smooth, but Jack's pulse quickened as the doors opened to reveal the plush carpeted hallway. Two guards flanked the entrance to Room 1203, their posture rigid, their earpieces faintly glowing under the soft light.

Jack stopped just short of the guards, leaning casually against the wall as he adjusted his cufflinks. Through his earpiece, Irina's voice was a whisper. "Distraction in three… two… one."

A faint beep echoed down the hallway, followed by a small puff of smoke from an air vent near the ceiling. The guards' heads snapped up, their hands instinctively moving toward their weapons as they turned to investigate.

Jack moved quickly, slipping past them and unlocking the door with a swipe of Irina's portable hacking device.

THE SUITE WAS a luxurious command center. A conference table dominated the space, its surface covered in financial documents, tablets, and a holographic projector displaying shipping routes and investment portfolios. At the head of the table stood Isaac Fontaine, his tailored suit immaculate, his expression calm and calculating.

Around the table sat five men, each exuding an air of power. Jack recognized two of them immediately—high-level financiers tied to The Veil's shadow network.

Irina slipped in beside Jack, her movements silent as she placed a listening device near the two-way mirror separating them from the meeting. "We'll record their discussion and extract the files from the control panel once they leave," she whispered.

Isaac's voice carried through the glass, smooth and deliberate. "The transfers will be finalized tonight. Once the funds are in motion, we'll destabilize key markets. By the time they recover, we'll have consolidated control."

One of the financiers, a portly man with a diamond-studded tie pin, leaned forward. "And the operatives in Paris and Berlin?"

Isaac's thin smile didn't waver. "In position. By morning, we'll have the leverage we need."

Jack's jaw tightened as he glanced at Irina. "They're not just funding chaos—they're orchestrating it."

Irina nodded, her green eyes hard. "We need to move now. The longer we wait, the closer they get to pulling the trigger."

JUST AS THEY prepared to breach the room, the door opened, and Maria Ortega stepped inside. Jack and Irina froze, their tension spiking as the EISA operative strode confidently to the head of the table.

"Maria," Isaac said with a faint smile. "Right on time."

Maria's voice was cold, her tone brooking no argument. "I don't like loose ends, Isaac. Is everything in place?"

"Of course," Isaac replied smoothly. "You'll find I'm quite efficient when properly motivated."

Jack's grip on his pistol tightened as he whispered, "She's not just complicit. She's running this."

Irina's voice was steady, but her words were edged with resolve. "If we take her out now, we risk exposing the entire operation."

"And if we don't?" Jack countered.

Irina's eyes didn't leave the scene beyond the glass. "Then we wait."

THE MEETING CONCLUDED MINUTES LATER, the financiers filing out one by one. Maria lingered, her sharp eyes sweeping the room before she exited through the main door.

Irina slipped into the suite first, her weapon drawn. Jack followed, moving quickly to the control panel. He plugged in a flash drive, his fingers flying over the keyboard as he began extracting the files.

The progress bar crawled forward, each second feeling like an eternity.

"Faster," Irina urged, keeping her eyes on the hallway.

"I'm not exactly downloading cat videos," Jack muttered, his voice taut.

The sound of approaching footsteps shattered the tension. Irina raised her weapon, her voice sharp. "We've got company."

THE GUARDS BURST in moments later, their guns raised. Irina fired first, her shots precise as she neutralized two of them. Jack moved to cover the doorway, his own weapon barking as the remaining guards returned fire.

The control panel chimed, signaling the completion of the download. Jack grabbed the flash drive, shoving it into his jacket. "Got it. Let's go!"

Irina dispatched the last guard with a sharp kick to the knee, her movements efficient and deadly.

"Exit plan?" Jack asked as they sprinted down the hallway.

Irina smirked faintly. "Follow me."

THEY SLIPPED INTO A SERVICE CORRIDOR, weaving through the maze of backrooms and stairwells until they reached the ground floor. The alarms began blaring just as they stepped out into the cold Vienna night.

Their waiting car sped toward them, and they climbed in without hesitation. Jack leaned back, exhaling sharply as he pulled out the flash drive.

"What did we get?" Irina asked, her voice steady despite the adrenaline.

Jack plugged the drive into his tablet, scanning the files. "Everything. Names, accounts, locations. This is Isaac's entire network."

Irina's expression didn't soften. "And Ortega?"

Jack's jaw tightened. "Enough to start a war. But not enough to finish it."

Irina nodded, her voice cold. "Then we keep going."

As the car disappeared into the Vienna streets, Jack and Irina both knew the stakes had never been higher—and the final confrontation was drawing closer.

CHAPTER 9
FINAL COUNTDOWN IN ISTANBUL

THE CITY of Istanbul sprawled beneath a midnight sky, alive with its timeless energy. The Golden Horn reflected the scattered lights of ships docked in the harbor, while the faint hum of activity emanated from the industrial port. On a crumbling rooftop overlooking the district, Jack Jones and Irina Stepanov crouched in silence, their breaths visible in the cold night air.

Through her binoculars, Irina scanned the warehouse below—a sprawling hub of steel and concrete, its perimeter patrolled by armed guards. The faint hum of cargo trucks and the clang of machinery carried through the stillness.

"That's it," she murmured, lowering the binoculars. "The nerve center of Isaac's operation."

Jack adjusted his tactical vest, his gaze fixed on the flickering lights in the distance. "And ground zero for The Veil's next move. Isaac, Herrick, and their team are all in there, plotting global chaos. It's almost like they want us to ruin their night."

Irina smirked faintly, checking her silenced pistol. "They won't make it easy."

Jack mirrored her smirk, though it didn't reach his eyes. "They never do."

THE MAZE of shipping containers and concrete walls loomed over Jack and Irina as they moved silently through the shadows. The air was thick with the scent of oil and saltwater, and the occasional rumble of a passing truck echoed in the distance.

Irina held up a hand, signaling for Jack to stop. "Two guards by the main gate," she whispered, pointing to the figures silhouetted by a flickering floodlight.

Jack nodded, gripping his knife. "We take them out quietly. The less noise, the better."

The guards didn't see it coming. Jack dispatched the first with a swift chokehold, while Irina neutralized the second with a precise blow to the temple. They dragged the unconscious bodies behind a stack of crates before slipping deeper into the compound.

THE INTERIOR of the warehouse was cavernous, its high ceilings amplifying every sound. Stacks of crates lined the walls, many of them marked with Cyrillic lettering and international shipping codes. A group of armed operatives patrolled the floor, their movements methodical.

In the center of the space stood Isaac Fontaine. He loomed over a metal table strewn with maps, monitors, and laptops, flanked by Markus Herrick and a Veil emissary—a tall, shadowed figure with an aura of cold authority.

Jack and Irina watched from a darkened corner, their comms syncing with a transmitter Irina had planted earlier. The audio feed crackled to life.

"The final shipment leaves tomorrow," Isaac said, his voice calm and commanding. "Berlin, Paris, and Rome. Everything is in place."

Herrick frowned, his skepticism evident. "And Jones and Stepanov? They've survived longer than expected."

Isaac's smile was razor-sharp. "Our associates are dealing with them as we speak. By the time the markets open, they'll be irrelevant."

Jack clenched his fists, his eyes meeting Irina's. "Always nice to be appreciated."

Irina's gaze was cold. "We can't wait any longer. We take them now."

JACK FIRED THE FIRST SHOT, silencing one of the guards before the room erupted into chaos. Irina moved like a shadow, her silenced pistol dispatching targets with ruthless efficiency as they pushed toward the table.

Isaac's operatives reacted quickly, diving for cover and returning fire. The warehouse transformed into a battlefield, the cacophony of gunfire and shouted orders filling the air.

"Stay close!" Jack called out, dodging behind a stack of crates as bullets whizzed past.

"I'm not going anywhere," Irina shot back, reloading her weapon.

Amid the chaos, Isaac and Herrick retreated through a side door, their movements deliberate and unhurried.

"They're running," Jack growled, his frustration evident.

Irina's jaw tightened. "Not for long."

THE ADJOINING WAREHOUSE was a labyrinth of conveyor belts and assembly lines. At the far end of the room, Isaac stood with his pistol drawn, his calm demeanor a stark contrast to the chaos unfolding around him.

"Jones," Isaac called out, his voice cutting through the noise. "Always the predictable one."

Jack leveled his weapon at him, his smirk faint but steady. "And you're always the coward running to your next hiding place."

Isaac's smile didn't falter. "Running? Hardly. I'm simply moving the pieces on the board. Something you've never been very good at."

Before Jack could respond, Herrick stepped into view, his weapon trained on Irina.

"Drop it," Herrick barked.

Jack hesitated, his pistol wavering.

"Do it," Isaac ordered, his tone unyielding. "Or she dies."

Irina's eyes met Jack's, her voice steady. "Don't."

BEFORE HERRICK COULD REACT, Irina moved. She dropped to the ground, sweeping Herrick's legs out from under him. His weapon clattered to the floor as Jack fired, grazing Isaac's arm and forcing him to retreat.

Herrick scrambled to recover, but Irina pinned him with a swift knee to his chest, wrenching his arms behind him.

Isaac, clutching his wounded arm, smirked as he backed toward the exit. "This isn't over, Jones."

"It is for you," Jack growled, advancing.

But Isaac reached for a detonator clipped to his belt, pressing it without hesitation.

A DEAFENING EXPLOSION rocked the building, sending crates and machinery tumbling. Jack grabbed Irina, pulling her behind a steel beam as debris rained down around them.

"He's rigged the place," Irina said, coughing through the dust. "We need to move."

Jack nodded, his jaw tight. "Not without the data."

They scrambled toward the central table, where a battered laptop blinked with a transmission in progress. Jack's stomach sank as he saw the files being uploaded—dossiers, financial records, and deployment plans all marked with logos from EISA and NESA.

"This isn't intel," Irina said, her tone sharp. "It's a smear campaign."

Jack slammed the laptop shut, his voice bitter. "He's framing us and burning every bridge we have."

The faint sound of Isaac's laughter echoed through the speakers.

"You wanted to stop me, Jones? Congratulations—you've just made yourself the enemy of everyone."

As THE BUILDING began to collapse, Jack and Irina sprinted toward the exit, dragging Herrick with them. They emerged into the freezing night air just as the warehouse imploded, flames licking the sky.

Jack leaned against a shipping container, catching his breath. "We've got the files, but he's put a target on our backs."

Irina nodded, her gaze hard. "Then we stop running. We expose The Veil, Isaac, and everyone who's helped them."

Jack's smirk returned, faint but resolute. "Let's make sure they regret underestimating us."

As the first light of dawn broke over Istanbul, they disappeared into the shadows, the final battle looming on the horizon.

CHAPTER 10
INTO THE SHADOWS

THE SAFE HOUSE was perched deep within a dense forest, its isolation marked by silence save for the whisper of wind through the trees. A damp chill seeped through the cabin's rough wooden walls, carrying the faint scent of pine and decay. The interior was sparse— just a table, two chairs, and a flickering lantern casting long shadows.

Jack Jones leaned over a map of Europe spread across the table, his blue eyes locked on the red circles and black lines crisscrossing the paper. Each mark represented a city, a shipment, or a potential target linked to Isaac Fontaine's network. His fingers drummed against the table, the rhythmic tapping a rare sign of his agitation.

Irina Stepanov leaned against the wall, her arms crossed and her sharp green eyes fixed on Jack. She'd grown used to his relentless focus, but tonight, the weight of the mission seemed to press harder than ever.

"You've been staring at that map for hours," she said, breaking the silence.

Jack didn't look up. "Because I'm trying to figure out Isaac's next move. If we miss it, this whole thing starts over."

Irina stepped closer, her voice steady but firm. "We already know the targets. Berlin, Paris, and Rome. We disrupt the shipments, take out the leadership, and the network crumbles."

Jack's frustration flashed as he finally looked at her. "You really think that'll be enough? Isaac's like a hydra. Cut off one head, and another grows in its place."

Irina placed a hand on the map, her fingers brushing one of the circles. "Then we go after The Veil. Isaac is dangerous, but he's just a piece of their machine. We dismantle their leadership, their funding, their infrastructure. Without them, he's nothing."

Jack leaned back in his chair, his smirk humorless. "Sure. And where do we find them? The Veil doesn't exactly post their addresses online."

Irina's lips curved into a faint smile. "They don't need to. The files from Vienna pointed to offshore accounts. It's all connected—Zurich's financial district. We follow the money, and it'll lead us straight to them."

Jack arched a brow. "Zurich, huh? Sounds like a cozy vacation spot."

"If by cozy you mean crawling with mercenaries and double agents," Irina replied. "Pack light."

THE QUIET OF the cabin was shattered by a distant rumble. Jack tensed, moving to the window as the faint glow of headlights pierced the darkness between the trees.

"We've got company," he muttered, reaching for his pistol.

Irina grabbed her bag, her expression calm but sharp. "They're early. Isaac's men must've tracked us from Istanbul."

A rapid knock on the door made them freeze. Jack raised his weapon, his voice low. "Friends of yours?"

The door opened cautiously, revealing Dimitri Valenko, his coat soaked from the rain. The arms dealer's usual smirk was absent, replaced by a grim urgency.

"We need to move," Dimitri said, his accent thick. "Now."

Jack didn't lower his weapon. "You alone?"

"Do I look like I'd bring guests?" Dimitri shot back, stepping inside. "Isaac's people are closing in. Ten minutes, maybe less."

THE TRIO SLIPPED into the forest, their movements silent and precise. The glow of approaching vehicles flickered between the trees, accompanied by the low rumble of engines.

Dimitri led the way, his pace brisk as they navigated the uneven terrain. "There's a helicopter in a clearing two clicks north. It'll get you to Zurich."

"And you?" Jack asked, his tone sharp.

Dimitri smirked faintly. "I'll catch up. Someone needs to slow them down."

Irina hesitated, her green eyes narrowing. "You're playing the hero now?"

Dimitri's expression hardened. "Let's just say I have a vested interest in keeping you alive. Now go."

Jack nodded, his voice steady. "Don't do anything stupid, Dimitri."

The arms dealer gave a mock salute before disappearing into the shadows.

BY THE TIME Jack and Irina reached the clearing, the faint glow of dawn was breaking through the treetops. The helicopter's rotors spun furiously, kicking up a whirlwind of leaves and debris.

As they climbed aboard, Jack leaned out to take one last look at the forest, his gaze lingering on the distant headlights.

"He'll make it," Irina said, her tone softer than usual.

Jack nodded, though his expression remained tense. "Let's make sure we do, too."

THE CABIN of the helicopter was filled with the steady hum of the engine, a sound that seemed to amplify the weight of their thoughts. Jack leaned against the wall, his eyes closed, while Irina worked methodically on her laptop, reviewing the intel they'd gathered.

A faint buzz drew Jack's attention. He pulled a satellite phone from his pocket, hesitating before dialing.

Irina glanced at him. "Calling for backup?"

Jack shook his head. "Something more important."

After a few rings, a familiar voice answered.

"Jack?" Amy's tone was cautious, a mix of relief and frustration.

"Yeah, it's me," Jack said, his voice softer than usual. "Just... wanted to check in."

There was a pause. "You okay?"

Jack let out a dry laugh. "Not really. But I'm trying to be."

Amy's voice softened. "You don't have to do this alone, you know."

Jack's gaze shifted to Irina, who was focused on her screen. "I'm starting to realize that."

AS THE HELICOPTER descended over Zurich's financial district, the city's sleek skyscrapers glinted in the morning light. Jack and Irina exchanged a glance, their resolve unspoken but mutual.

"This is it," Jack said, securing his gear. "Time to cut the head off the snake."

Irina nodded, her expression unreadable. "Let's make it count."

The helicopter touched down on a rooftop, and as they stepped out, the weight of their mission pressed down harder than ever. Zurich was a city of order and precision, but Jack and Irina were about to bring chaos into its heart.

The fight wasn't over. It was just beginning.

The End

DEEP COVER

A SHORT THRILLER

CHAPTER 1
INTO THE SYNDICATE

THE BALKAN DOCKYARD stretched like a labyrinth along the Adriatic, its rusted shipping containers stacked in precarious towers beneath looming cranes. The low hum of machinery mixed with the steady rhythm of waves lapping against the docks, while floodlights painted everything in shades of cold white and deep shadow. At first glance, it seemed like an ordinary scene of commerce—grimy workers hauling crates, forklifts trundling back and forth. But to Jack Jones, it was a stage for deception.

From the shadows near the perimeter fence, Jack adjusted his worn jacket, his sharp blue eyes scanning every detail. He saw the truth beneath the surface. The dock's activity was too carefully choreographed, the workers' movements too precise. The crates bore no logos or markings, just a coded series of numbers stenciled in black—a quiet nod to the cargo's illegitimacy.

"This is Fontaine's operation, all right," Jack muttered, his voice barely above a whisper.

A crackle in his earpiece pulled him from his thoughts. Irina Stepanov's voice came through, low and steady. "What do you see?"

"Smuggling route. Arms shipments, maybe more," Jack replied. "And guards. Lots of guards."

The heavy fog thickened as Jack moved along the dockyard,

obscuring the floodlights and muffling the machinery's clatter. A sudden tremor beneath his feet made him freeze—a faint vibration, rhythmic and unnatural. He crouched, pressing a hand to the ground. His expression hardened.

"Underground tunnel," he muttered into the comm.

Irina's response was sharp. "What are they moving that requires this level of stealth?"

"Nothing good," Jack replied. "I'll check it out."

He slipped into the shadows, finding a metal hatch partially obscured by crates. As he pried it open, a hiss of compressed air sent a chill up his spine. Below, a hidden freight elevator descended into the depths.

"Jack," Irina warned, her tone urgent. "Reinforcements heading your way. This might not be the time to play archaeologist."

Jack smirked, lowering himself into the shaft. "You've got my back, don't you?"

Across the dockyard, Irina perched on a stack of crates, her dark leather jacket and boots giving her the air of someone who belonged. She lounged as if bored, but her sharp green eyes flicked between the main office and the loading zones, cataloging every detail.

"Good. You're supposed to look like you're useful. Try not to make it too convincing," she added.

Jack's smirk widened. "I'll do my best."

JACK'S ENTRANCE to the main gate was anything but subtle. He walked with deliberate confidence, hands visible at his sides, every step declaring he had nothing to lose. The guards stiffened, their hands moving instinctively to their weapons.

"Can we help you?" the closest one barked, his broad shoulders filling the space between the steel bars.

Jack tilted his head, his smirk faint. "Depends. I'm looking for work."

The guard's brow furrowed. "Work?"

"Word around the docks is Fontaine's looking for muscle," Jack said, his tone casual but sharp enough to carry authority. "I've got references, if you need them."

The guard exchanged a glance with his partner. "We don't just let anyone walk in."

Jack's smile didn't waver. "You'd be smart to make an exception."

Before the guard could reply, Jack lunged forward, grabbing his wrist and twisting it sharply. The man's pistol clattered to the ground as Jack yanked him off balance, slamming him into the gate.

"See?" Jack said, his tone almost friendly. "I'm handy in a fight."

The second guard reached for his weapon, but Jack turned sharply, leveling a warning glare. "Don't. I'd hate to ruin a perfectly good first impression."

After a tense moment, the second guard lowered his hand.

"All right," the first guard muttered, rubbing his wrist. "Follow me. But if you're lying, you won't leave here alive."

Jack smirked, adjusting his jacket. "Looking forward to the interview."

MEANWHILE, Irina worked a different angle. Near the main office, she struck up a conversation with Dmitry Koval, a wiry man with darting eyes and an air of perpetual unease. The local smuggler reeked of opportunism—someone used to skimming profits and covering his tracks.

"You're bold, showing up here," Dmitry said, suspicion thick in his voice.

Irina shrugged, the faintest hint of a smile on her lips. "I could say the same about you. Skimming off Fontaine's shipments? Risky business."

Dmitry stiffened. "Who told you that?"

"Relax," Irina said lightly, brushing an imaginary speck of dust from her sleeve. "I'm not here to out you. I'm here because Fontaine's network needs people who can think for themselves. People who see opportunities."

Dmitry's brow furrowed. "What kind of opportunities?"

Irina leaned in, her voice dropping to a conspiratorial whisper. "The kind that make us both rich—and keep Fontaine from noticing."

Dmitry hesitated, his gaze searching hers for any sign of deception. Finally, he nodded. "All right. What do you need?"

INSIDE THE SPRAWLING WAREHOUSE, Jack was introduced to Anton Karpov. The lieutenant exuded cold precision, his tailored suit and slicked-back hair a stark contrast to the grimy surroundings. Karpov's pale blue eyes studied Jack with surgical detachment, sizing him up like a tool.

"So, you're the new muscle," Karpov said flatly.

"Looks that way," Jack replied.

"Prove it," Karpov said, nodding toward a heavy crate. "Get that onto the truck."

Jack arched a brow. "That's it? I thought you wanted to see if I could fight."

Karpov's lips curved into a thin smile. "You'll fight soon enough. For now, just do what you're told."

Jack nodded, stepping toward the crate. He pretended to strain as he lifted it, using the opportunity to scan the room—cataloging security cameras and the patterns of the guards' movements.

As he loaded the crate onto the truck, Karpov gave a curt nod. "Good enough. You'll do for now."

HOURS LATER, Jack patrolled the dockyard, his steps careful but unhurried. The darkness was thick, floodlights casting long shadows over the containers. His earpiece crackled softly, and Irina's voice came through, low and clear.

"Status?"

"Made it in," Jack murmured. "Karpov thinks I'm dumb muscle. What about you?"

"Dmitry's chatty," Irina replied. "Fontaine's planning a major shipment in three days. Details are vague, but it's big."

Jack frowned. "Big how?"

Irina's tone was dry. "Big enough to get us both killed if we don't figure it out."

Jack's faint chuckle echoed softly as he reached a stack of crates marked with the same coded numbers he'd seen earlier. "Sounds like we're off to a great start. Try not to blow your cover, okay?"

"Funny," Irina said. "I was about to tell you the same thing."

Jack's smile faded as he disappeared into the shadows, the weight of their mission pressing down on him. For now, they were still in the game. But Jack knew better than anyone how quickly the odds could change.

CHAPTER 2
SEPARATE PATHS

THE MORNING LIGHT filtered weakly through the haze over the coastline, casting the Balkan dockyard in muted grays and blues. The air carried a biting chill, mingling with the faint scent of diesel and salt. Jack Jones leaned against a stack of pallets at the edge of the dock, watching workers move crates onto a barge. His role as a hired enforcer held firm—for now.

Karpov's voice barked through the warehouse doors behind him. "Jones! You're up."

Jack straightened, keeping his expression neutral as he walked toward the warehouse. Inside, the fluorescent lights buzzed faintly, illuminating the cavernous space. The clatter of machinery and shouted orders created a chaotic backdrop.

"What's the job?" Jack asked casually, approaching Karpov.

The lieutenant turned, his stony gaze sweeping over Jack like a scanner. "We're testing loyalty today. New blood needs to prove their worth."

Jack raised an eyebrow. "How?"

Karpov gestured toward a corner of the warehouse, where a group of men sat around a table playing cards. Their scarred faces and tattooed arms spoke of hard lives and rough work.

"You're vetting recruits," Karpov said. "One of them's been feeding intel to the wrong people. I want you to figure out which one and take care of it."

Jack's stomach tightened, though he kept his face unreadable. "Interrogate them?"

Karpov's thin smile carried no warmth. "If that's what you want to call it."

Meanwhile, Irina Stepanov worked a different angle. She sat in the corner of the main office, a small laptop open in front of her as she typed with deliberate efficiency. Her role as an information broker required balance—valuable enough to earn Fontaine's trust, yet unassuming enough to avoid suspicion.

A shadow fell across her desk, and Irina glanced up to see Dmitry Koval leaning against the doorframe. He held a steaming cup of coffee, which he offered with a faint smirk.

"Thought you might need a pick-me-up," he said.

Irina accepted the cup, her expression impassive. "Generous of you."

"Call it self-preservation," Dmitry said, settling into the chair across from her. "You're my insurance policy, remember?"

Irina returned to her typing, her voice light. "Then maybe you should let me work."

Dmitry chuckled, but his eyes narrowed as he leaned forward. "Fontaine's keeping something big under wraps. The shipment you asked about? No one's talking. Not even Karpov."

Irina's fingers paused briefly on the keyboard. "That's because it's important. Keep listening."

Dmitry shook his head. "Careful, Stepanov. People who listen too much around here don't last long."

Irina met his gaze, her green eyes hard. "Neither do people who stop listening. Remember that."

BACK IN THE WAREHOUSE, Jack approached the card table, his steps measured. The recruits barely acknowledged him, their focus locked on the pile of cash and coins in the center of the table.

"Break time's over," Jack said, his tone sharp.

One of the men, a burly figure with a scar running down his cheek, smirked. "You Fontaine's new errand boy?"

Jack didn't react, his gaze sweeping over the group. "One of you's been talking to the wrong people. Karpov wants it handled."

The tension at the table thickened. The recruits exchanged wary glances.

The scarred man leaned back, his smirk fading. "What makes you think it's one of us?"

Jack pulled out his pistol, spinning it idly in his hand. "Doesn't matter what I think. Only matters what Karpov thinks. So, who's got something to say?"

No one moved.

Jack sighed, aiming the pistol at the nearest recruit. "Guess we'll do this the hard way."

The man flinched, raising his hands. "Wait! It's not me!"

Jack's icy gaze shifted to the next recruit. "You? Got something to share?"

The scarred man stood abruptly, his chair scraping loudly against the floor. "This is bullshit!"

Jack moved in a blur, grabbing the man by the collar and slamming him against the wall. The recruit grunted, his eyes wide as Jack pressed the pistol against his chest.

"You seem nervous," Jack said, his voice low. "Why's that?"

"I'm not—"

Jack twisted the man's collar tighter. "Lying gets you nowhere. Talk."

The man's bravado crumbled, his voice trembling. "Fine! I've been selling scraps to the Serbians! Just leftovers from the shipments, nothing big."

Jack released him, stepping back with a look of disdain. "Stupid. But not the intel leak we're looking for."

Before the man could respond, Jack turned to Karpov, who had been watching silently from the shadows. "Your call. But he's small-time."

Karpov nodded. "Fair assessment. Let's see how long his luck holds."

HOURS LATER, Jack and Irina found a moment alone near the dockyard's storage containers. Jack leaned against the cool metal, his expression tight as he rubbed his temples.

"Karpov's testing me," he muttered. "Gave me a loyalty check, had me vet recruits. One guy cracked, but he wasn't the leak they're looking for."

Irina studied him, her voice measured. "Karpov doesn't trust anyone. It's his way of keeping everyone under control."

Jack smirked faintly. "Sounds like your kind of guy."

Irina ignored the jab, glancing toward the main warehouse. "I've got Dmitry digging into the shipment. Whatever Fontaine's moving, it's big enough to keep everyone tight-lipped."

Jack's expression darkened. "Big enough to make this whole operation worth the risk."

Irina nodded, her voice quiet. "We need more. Karpov's loyal to Fontaine, but even he has limits. If we find those, we can use them."

Jack straightened, his smirk fading. "And if we can't?"

Irina's green eyes met his, steady and unwavering. "Then we improvise. Like always."

CHAPTER 3
THE ARMS BAZAAR

THE UNDERGROUND AUCTION took place in the basement of a defunct opera house, its faded grandeur overshadowed by an air of quiet menace. Massive crystal chandeliers still hung from the ceiling, their flickering light casting strange shadows on the ornate plaster walls. Rows of folding chairs faced a stage, where crates of illicit goods —ranging from firearms to high-tech surveillance equipment—were displayed like art at a gallery opening.

Jack Jones adjusted the cuff of his suit jacket, his eyes scanning the crowd. It was a mix of hardened criminals, well-dressed intermediaries, and cold-eyed buyers who avoided small talk. In the center of it all, Isaac Fontaine loomed without needing to stand, his reputation cutting through the chatter like a blade.

On the far side of the room, Irina Stepanov stood near a table lined with champagne flutes. Her navy evening gown fit the occasion perfectly, though the sharpness in her green eyes set her apart from the idle elegance around her.

"You look like you're enjoying yourself," Jack murmured into the concealed mic in his lapel.

Irina didn't glance his way, her fingers brushing the edge of a glass as she replied. "And you look like you're about to get shot."

Jack smirked faintly. "Just trying to fit in."

"Try harder," she said dryly, before turning her attention back to the room.

The auctioneer, a wiry man with a slick smile, clapped his hands to draw the crowd's attention. "Ladies and gentlemen, we begin tonight with a truly exceptional lot. Prototype drones, fresh from a manufacturing delay in Geneva. Lightweight, silent, and virtually undetectable."

Murmurs rippled through the crowd as the first crate was opened, revealing sleek black drones lined up like soldiers. Jack tensed slightly, noting the intense interest among the buyers.

"These aren't just toys," the auctioneer continued. "They're battlefield assets. Shall we start the bidding at two million euros?"

Jack's voice was low in the comm. "Isaac's stepping up his game. Those drones could shift the balance for anyone who gets their hands on them."

"Focus," Irina replied sharply. "Your job is to get close to Fontaine. Mine is to plant the bug."

Jack's smirk faded as his eyes found Isaac Fontaine, seated near the stage. The crime lord's sharp suit and calm demeanor gave him the air of a man completely in control, though his dark eyes scanned the room with predatory intent.

Irina moved through the crowd with practiced ease, her steps measured and graceful. As she passed a waiter carrying a tray of champagne, her hand brushed briefly against the edge of the tray. The waiter nodded imperceptibly and moved toward the stage, where the sound equipment sat behind a curtain.

"I'm in position," Irina murmured.

"Good," Jack replied. "Just don't get caught. These people don't hand out second chances."

"Funny," Irina said. "I was about to say the same to you."

As Irina planted the bug, Jack approached the edge of the stage. He caught the auctioneer's eye, raising a hand to signal interest in the drones. The move wasn't in the plan, but Jack's instincts told him it was the quickest way to draw Fontaine's attention.

"Ah, a bold bid!" the auctioneer exclaimed. "Do I hear two-point-five million?"

A sharp glance from Fontaine silenced the other bidders. The auctioneer hesitated but recovered quickly. "Sold, to our distinguished guest."

Jack offered a faint smile as the murmurs subsided. He knew he'd painted a target on his back, but that was the point.

As the crowd's attention shifted to the next lot, Jack felt a presence at his shoulder. He turned to find Fontaine standing beside him, his expression calm but calculating.

"You've got expensive tastes," Fontaine said, his voice smooth.

Jack shrugged. "When the product's worth it."

Fontaine's lips curved into a thin smile. "I'm not familiar with your name. New to this crowd?"

"Matt Daniels," Jack said, extending a hand. "Let's just say I've worked for people who prefer to stay out of the spotlight."

Fontaine didn't take the hand, his sharp eyes locking onto Jack's. "In my experience, people who avoid the spotlight usually have something to hide."

Jack smirked faintly. "Don't we all?"

The silence stretched before Fontaine finally nodded. "Enjoy the evening. I'll be watching."

As Fontaine moved away, Jack exhaled slowly. "Well, that went great."

Irina's voice crackled through his earpiece, dry and sharp. "You're lucky he didn't kill you on the spot."

The evening wore on, the auction's intensity growing as bigger and more dangerous items took the stage. Irina remained near the edge of the room, her attention divided between the auction and Fontaine's movements. The bug she'd planted transmitted clearly, fragments of conversation filtering through her earpiece.

"Shipment's secure," one voice said.

"Coordinates locked," another added.

Irina's grip on her clutch tightened as she pieced it together. Fontaine's drones weren't just for sale—they were part of something bigger.

"Jack," her voice came through, low and urgent. "We've got a problem."

She turned just as a heavyset man in a dark suit stepped into her path, his hand clamping down on her arm.

"Mr. Fontaine would like a word," the man said.

Jack saw the interaction from across the room, his jaw tightening. Fontaine wasn't a man who tolerated loose ends, and Irina's cover was dangerously thin.

"Stay calm," Irina said quietly.

"Calm?" Jack muttered. "You're walking into the lion's den."

"And you're going to make sure I walk out," Irina replied.

IN A BACK ROOM, Fontaine stood by a small table, his gaze icy as he studied Irina.

"You're an interesting addition to tonight's crowd," he said. "My people tell me you've been asking questions. Care to explain?"

Irina didn't flinch. "I'm an information broker. It's my job to ask questions."

Fontaine tilted his head slightly. "And your job ends where my patience begins."

Before he could press further, the door burst open. Jack strode in, pistol drawn.

"Sorry to interrupt," Jack said, his voice cold. "But I think this meeting's over."

Fontaine's lips curved into a smile, but his eyes burned with fury. "You're making a mistake."

Jack smirked faintly. "It wouldn't be my first."

He grabbed Irina's arm, pulling her toward the door as Fontaine's men scrambled.

THE CHAOS of their escape echoed through the opera house as they pushed through the crowd. By the time they reached the exit, Jack's mind was already racing.

The moment they hit the alley behind the opera house, an explosion rocked the ground beneath their feet, sending a plume of debris into the air. Jack shielded Irina instinctively as shards of glass rained down.

"That wasn't us," Jack said, coughing as he steadied her.

"No," Irina replied, her eyes narrowing. "Fontaine's covering his tracks."

Above them, shadows moved across the rooftops, and Jack's heart sank. "Snipers," he muttered. "We're boxed in."

Irina scanned their surroundings, her mind racing. "The canal. There's an old service tunnel two blocks west."

"Great," Jack said, firing a shot at the advancing guards. "You lead; I'll entertain our guests."

"That bug better be worth it," he muttered.

Irina's voice was steady despite her quick steps. "It'll lead us to Fontaine's next move. That's all that matters."

Jack nodded, his smirk faint. "Then let's make it count."

CHAPTER 4
CRACKS IN THE FAÇADE

THE ADRIATIC COASTLINE shimmered in the late afternoon sun, its jagged cliffs and turquoise waters forming a postcard-perfect backdrop for the fortress-like estate perched atop the hills. The sprawling mansion, a blend of modern glass and ancient stone, was a testament to Isaac Fontaine's wealth and influence. Armed guards patrolled the grounds, their movements precise and deliberate, while cameras swept the perimeter like unblinking eyes.

Jack Jones sat in the back seat of a sleek black SUV, his jaw tight as the vehicle ascended the winding driveway. Dressed in a sharp black suit, he looked every bit the high-level security operative Fontaine's organization needed. But beneath the tailored exterior, his mind churned with calculations and contingencies.

"Pull it together," he muttered under his breath. "One wrong move, and you're out—permanently."

IN A PRIVATE ROOM near the mansion's west wing, Irina Stepanov was playing a different game. She stood before a massive glass window overlooking the sea, her posture poised as if she belonged. Beside her, a tall, dark-haired woman in a crimson dress sipped champagne, her lips curving into a faint smile.

"Fontaine likes you," the woman said, her voice low and musical. "But he's not an easy man to impress."

Irina turned slightly, her green eyes cool and assessing. "I don't need to impress him. I just need him to see my value."

The woman tilted her head, studying Irina. "You don't scare easily, do you?"

Irina's lips curved faintly. "I can't afford to."

Their conversation was interrupted by the faint buzz of Irina's concealed earpiece. Jack's voice came through, low and dry. "Tell me you're not drinking with Fontaine's people."

"Relax," Irina murmured, barely moving her lips. "Just blending in. What's your status?"

"Inside," Jack replied. "Karpov's giving me the grand tour."

Jack's tour wasn't exactly leisurely. Anton Karpov, Fontaine's lieutenant, strode through the estate like a man with a permanent grudge, his pale blue eyes darting to every shadow.

"You'll report directly to me," Karpov said, his tone clipped. "Fontaine expects loyalty above all else. If you can't deliver that, you won't last long."

Jack smirked faintly. "I think I'll manage."

They stopped near a cluster of shipping containers on the edge of the property. Karpov gestured to the crates, his gaze sharp. "You're responsible for these. Fontaine's latest shipment. If anything goes wrong, it's on you."

Jack stepped closer, his fingers brushing the edge of the nearest container. The faint scent of chemicals wafted through the air, twisting his stomach as he recognized its significance.

"What's in them?" Jack asked, keeping his tone casual.

"Not your concern," Karpov replied, his voice cold. "Your job is to make sure they get where they're going."

LATER THAT EVENING, Jack and Irina stole a moment alone in a secluded hallway near the estate's east wing, their voices barely above a whisper.

"You're right," Jack said, his expression grim. "Something big's going down. The crates in the west yard? They're not just weapons. There's biochem gear in there—enough to take out entire cities if it's weaponized."

Irina's jaw tightened, though her voice remained steady. "And Fontaine's not the type to stockpile. He's moving it soon."

Jack leaned against the wall, rubbing the back of his neck. "Karpov's breathing down my neck, and Fontaine's got eyes everywhere. If we don't play this perfectly, we're screwed."

Irina glanced around, her instincts on high alert. "We're already screwed. We just haven't felt it yet."

Jack smirked faintly. "Comforting."

Irina's expression softened slightly, her voice dropping. "Look, stay close to Karpov. If he's running security for this operation, he knows where the shipments are going."

Jack nodded, his smirk fading. "And you? What's your next move?"

"I'll keep working Dmitry," Irina replied. "He's nervous. If anyone cracks under pressure, it'll be him."

THE NEXT DAY, Jack's instincts were tested when one of the estate guards confronted him near the shipping containers. The man, a stocky figure with a scar running across his cheek, looked at Jack with open suspicion.

"You're new," the guard said. "How'd you get in so fast?"

Jack raised an eyebrow, his tone sharp. "I didn't 'get in.' I earned my way here. You got a problem with that?"

The guard stepped closer, his posture aggressive. "Just saying,

Fontaine doesn't like outsiders. You screw this up, you won't get a second chance."

Jack held his ground, his blue eyes locked onto the man's. "Thanks for the warning. Now get out of my way."

The tension crackled between them for a long moment before the guard finally stepped aside.

Meanwhile, Irina worked Dmitry with her usual precision, her every word and gesture calculated to keep him talking.

"It's all happening too fast," Dmitry said, his voice a low whisper. "Fontaine's got Karpov running around like a madman, and now there's talk of another meeting—something big."

Irina leaned in slightly, her tone feigning curiosity. "A meeting with who?"

Dmitry hesitated, his nervous gaze darting around the room. "Some of The Veil's people. I don't know names, but if they're coming here, it means Fontaine's about to take this operation to the next level."

Irina's pulse quickened. "When?"

"Tonight," Dmitry said. "But that's all I know. I swear."

Irina patted his arm, her smile faint. "You've been very helpful, Dmitry. I'll make sure Fontaine appreciates your loyalty."

That evening, the estate buzzed with quiet activity as the meeting began. Jack and Irina stayed on opposite sides of the operation, each playing their role while carefully avoiding detection.

From his vantage point near the shipping containers, Jack watched sleek black cars arrive one by one, each carrying a figure more dangerous than the last.

Inside, Irina positioned herself near the main hall, her earpiece crackling faintly as she relayed updates to Jack.

"This is it," she murmured. "Fontaine's inner circle. We need to hear what they're planning."

Jack's voice was tight. "Then let's hope your bug is working."

As the meeting unfolded, the weight of the operation became clear. Fontaine wasn't just moving weapons or chemicals—he was coordinating a multi-pronged attack designed to destabilize key European cities.

Jack and Irina listened in silence, their shared realization sinking in: this wasn't just a mission anymore. It was a race against time.

CHAPTER 5
THE VEIL REVEALED

THE SECLUDED MOUNTAIN villa stood in stark contrast to the sprawling dockyards and opulent mansions of Fontaine's usual haunts. Perched high in the Balkans, its isolated position offered both security and secrecy, with a panoramic view of the mist-shrouded valleys below. Part luxury retreat, part fortress, the villa's thick stone walls, bulletproof windows, and patrolling guards betrayed its true purpose.

Jack Jones leaned against a weathered stone railing on the terrace, his sharp blue eyes scanning the courtyard below. The faint rustle of leaves and the distant hum of generators were the only sounds in the crisp mountain air. Fontaine's people were on edge, their movements more deliberate than usual. Whatever was happening inside, it wasn't business as usual.

"You're quiet," Irina's voice crackled softly through Jack's concealed earpiece.

Jack didn't respond immediately. From his vantage point, he could see Anton Karpov in the courtyard, directing the arrival of black SUVs. The vehicles were unmarked, their tinted windows concealing passengers who didn't want to be seen.

"Guests are arriving," Jack said finally. "Looks like the VIP list just got longer."

INSIDE THE VILLA, Irina Stepanov played her role to perfection. Dressed in sleek, understated elegance, she moved through the gathering like a shadow, her sharp green eyes absorbing every detail. Conversations buzzed around her—fragments of deals, veiled threats, and cryptic remarks about Fontaine's latest plans.

She paused near the edge of the main hall, her gaze following a tall, broad-shouldered man with a military bearing as he joined Fontaine in the villa's private lounge. The man's presence exuded authority, his movements deliberate and his face unreadable. Irina's concealed earpiece buzzed faintly.

"Do you see him?" Jack asked.

"Just entered the lounge," Irina murmured, her tone measured. "Heavy security. I don't recognize him."

"That's because he's not local," Jack replied. "That's one of The Veil's emissaries. We're getting close."

Irina allowed herself a faint smile as she moved toward the lounge, weaving through the crowd with practiced ease. "Then it's time to find out what they're hiding."

THE PRIVATE LOUNGE was a study in contrasts—plush leather chairs and antique bookshelves against walls reinforced with hidden steel panels. Isaac Fontaine stood near the fireplace, his sharp suit and calm demeanor masking the ruthlessness that lay beneath.

Beside him, the emissary spoke in low tones, his voice clipped and precise.

"Our operatives are in place," the man said. "The assets will move within seventy-two hours. Once the infrastructure is compromised, the resulting chaos will pave the way for Phase Two."

Fontaine nodded, his dark eyes gleaming. "And the targets?"

"Berlin, Paris, Rome," the emissary replied. "Coordinated strikes on key facilities. Maximum disruption."

Irina's hand tightened briefly around the stem of the wine glass she carried. The pieces clicked into place—Fontaine wasn't just selling weapons. He was orchestrating a coordinated attack to destabilize Europe.

IN THE COURTYARD, Jack's patience was wearing thin. The increased activity and cryptic mentions of "assets" set his instincts on edge. As Karpov barked orders to the guards, Jack moved closer, keeping his steps casual but deliberate.

"Need a hand?" Jack asked, his tone light.

Karpov turned, his pale blue eyes narrowing. "Not unless you've suddenly become indispensable."

Jack smirked. "Just trying to earn my keep."

Karpov studied him for a moment before gesturing toward a row of crates near one of the SUVs. "Fine. Those need loading. And don't waste time."

Jack nodded, moving toward the crates. As he hefted the first one onto the truck, a familiar chemical scent hit him—sharp and acrid, unmistakable.

"Biochemicals," Jack muttered under his breath.

IRINA SLIPPED OUT of the lounge, her steps measured as she headed toward the villa's service corridor. Her earpiece buzzed faintly as she spoke. "Fontaine and The Veil are moving assets in seventy-two hours. Multiple targets—major cities. Jack, we need that shipment manifest."

"I'm working on it," Jack replied, his voice low. "But these crates? They're loaded with biochem gear. This isn't just about weapons—it's about scale."

Irina's pulse quickened as she processed his words. "Then we need to move fast. I'll create a distraction. Get that manifest and get out."

The distraction came sooner than Jack expected.

From his position in the courtyard, he saw a flash of light near the villa's west wing, followed by the blaring of alarms. Guards shouted orders, their voices cutting through the chaos as they scrambled to secure the perimeter.

Jack moved quickly, using the confusion to slip into the nearby storage facility. The room was dimly lit, its walls lined with rows of filing cabinets and digital terminals.

He found the manifest on one of the terminals, his fingers flying over the keyboard as he transferred the data onto a portable drive. His earpiece crackled again.

"Status?" Irina asked.

"Got it," Jack replied, tucking the drive into his jacket. "But the clock's ticking. You'd better be ready to run."

As Jack exited the storage facility, he nearly collided with Karpov. The lieutenant's cold gaze locked onto him, suspicion flashing across his face.

"What are you doing here?" Karpov demanded.

Jack's mind raced, his hand inching toward the concealed pistol at his waist. "Heard the commotion. Thought I'd make myself useful."

Karpov's eyes narrowed, weighing the excuse. "You're useful where I tell you to be. Get back to the crates."

Jack nodded, keeping his movements calm as he backed away. "On it."

The rendezvous point was a narrow trail leading away from the villa, hidden beneath dense trees. Jack reached it first, his breath steady despite the adrenaline coursing through his veins. Moments later, Irina appeared, her expression sharp but controlled.

"Everything's set," Jack said, holding up the drive. "Targets, schedules, the works."

Irina nodded, her green eyes blazing. "Then let's put it to use."

They disappeared into the shadows, leaving the villa behind. But the weight of what they'd uncovered lingered—a grim reminder of the stakes ahead.

CHAPTER 6
A FRAGILE ALLIANCE

THE SAFE HOUSE was tucked into the edge of a quiet village in Eastern Europe, its faded brick exterior blending seamlessly with a row of abandoned buildings. Inside, the room was dimly lit, the heavy curtains drawn tight against prying eyes. The central table was a battlefield of maps, a laptop, and printouts of the data Jack had pulled from the villa's storage facility.

Jack Jones sat in a chair with one leg propped on the table, scrolling through the manifest on the laptop. His sharp blue eyes flicked over the screen, his jaw tight as he processed the details. Every entry—a biochem shipment, a destination, a date—fit together in a grim mosaic.

"This isn't just sabotage," Jack said finally, his voice cutting through the tense silence. "It's systemic collapse. They're not hitting governments—they're hitting infrastructure. Water supplies, hospitals, power grids. Three cities in seventy-two hours."

Irina Stepanov stood near the window, her green eyes scanning the empty street below. Her posture was still, but the tension in her clasped hands betrayed the storm beneath her calm exterior.

"Berlin, Paris, and Rome," she said, her tone sharp. "Fontaine's playing a long game. This isn't about profit—it's about control."

Jack leaned back in his chair, running a hand through his hair.

"And The Veil's behind him, pulling the strings. Makes you wonder what their endgame is."

Irina's lips thinned, but she didn't reply. The weight of what they'd uncovered hung heavily in the room.

THE TENSION BROKE as the faint buzz of Irina's burner phone filled the air. She crossed the room, picking it up with quick precision. The voice on the other end was low and urgent.

"Stepanov," Dmitry said, his tone edged with fear. "You need to get out. Now. Karpov knows something's off—he's asking questions."

Irina's jaw tightened. "How much does he know?"

"Enough to be dangerous," Dmitry replied. "He's got people watching you and Jones. If you're still breathing, it's only because Fontaine hasn't given the order yet."

Irina's gaze flicked to Jack, who was already standing, his expression grim. "Thanks for the warning," she said before disconnecting the call.

Jack arched an eyebrow. "Friendly advice?"

"Karpov's onto us," Irina replied. "Dmitry says we're walking a razor's edge."

Jack smirked faintly, though it didn't reach his eyes. "Good to know where we stand."

THEIR CONVERSATION WAS INTERRUPTED by the sound of tires crunching on gravel. Irina moved to the window, her sharp gaze spotting a dark SUV pulling up outside the safe house.

"Unmarked," she murmured. "Three men. Armed."

Jack's hand went to his pistol as he moved toward the table, grabbing the laptop and shoving it into a bag. "They're not here for tea."

"Back door," Irina said, already moving.

The two operatives slipped out the back, their movements quick and silent. The alley behind the building was narrow and littered with debris, the faded graffiti on the walls a stark reminder of the area's desolation.

Voices echoed faintly from the front of the safe house as the men entered, their footsteps heavy on the creaking floorboards.

"We've got a window," Jack said, glancing at Irina. "But not a big one."

"Then move," she replied, her tone sharp.

THE VILLAGE STREETS WERE DESERTED, the faint glow of streetlights casting long shadows as Jack and Irina made their way toward the outskirts. Their steps were quick but measured, each corner taken with careful precision.

As they neared the edge of the village, the sound of an engine revving broke the stillness. A second SUV appeared at the far end of the street, its headlights sweeping toward them.

"Split up," Irina said, her voice low but firm.

Jack hesitated for a fraction of a second before nodding. "Meet at the rail yard."

Irina didn't wait for a response, disappearing down a narrow alley as Jack darted toward the opposite side of the street.

JACK MOVED through the shadows with practiced ease, his breathing steady despite the adrenaline coursing through his veins. He could hear the faint hum of the SUV's engine behind him, the soft crunch of tires on gravel growing louder.

He ducked into an old workshop, its broken windows and rusting tools offering little comfort. As the SUV rolled past, Jack pressed himself against the wall, his pistol drawn.

The vehicle slowed, its headlights sweeping the interior of the workshop. Jack's grip on the pistol tightened as one of the doors opened, a figure stepping out.

"Jones," the man called, his voice sharp. "We know you're here."

Jack's mind raced as he calculated his next move. His eyes locked onto a rusted wrench on the floor—heavy enough for what he had in mind.

As the man moved deeper into the workshop, Jack struck. The wrench connected with a dull thud, dropping the man silently to the floor. Quickly relieving the man of his weapon, Jack slipped out the back, his steps quick and quiet.

MEANWHILE, Irina navigated the narrow alleys with the precision of someone born to the shadows. She heard the faint voices of her pursuers, their frustration clear as they struggled to track her movements.

At the edge of the village, she spotted the rail yard—a sprawling expanse of rusting freight cars and overgrown tracks. She moved quickly, slipping between the train cars and finding cover behind a stack of wooden crates.

Moments later, Jack appeared, his breathing steady but his expression sharp.

"Nice timing," Irina said.

Jack smirked faintly. "Thought I'd let you start the party."

The two operatives regrouped, their attention shifting to the distant hum of engines. More vehicles were approaching, their headlights cutting through the darkness.

"We can't stay here," Irina said. "They'll have reinforcements soon."

Jack nodded, glancing at the freight cars. "Then we hitch a ride. These tracks lead to the next town, right?"

Irina's green eyes narrowed as she followed his gaze. "You're improvising."

"Always," Jack replied, moving toward one of the cars. "Come on."

THE FREIGHT CAR offered little comfort, its rusted interior cold and uninviting. But as the train began to move, the sound of pursuing engines faded into the distance.

Jack leaned against the wall, his breath finally slowing. "You were saying something about Karpov?"

Irina sat across from him, her expression unreadable. "He's more dangerous than we thought. And he's not the only one."

Jack smirked faintly. "What else is new?"

As the train rumbled through the night, the weight of their mission settled heavily between them. The fragile alliance they'd built was all that stood between them and disaster—and the cracks were already starting to show.

CHAPTER 7
INTO THE LION'S DEN

THE GLITTERING lights of Vienna stretched out like a tapestry beneath the clear winter sky, the city alive with the hum of nightlife. The grand ballroom of the Palais Reinhardt was no exception, its gilded chandeliers casting a warm glow over the gathering of Europe's elite. Beneath the veneer of opulence, whispers of power and danger moved through the crowd like an undercurrent.

Jack Jones adjusted his tie as he surveyed the room from the edge of the marble staircase. Dressed in a sleek black tuxedo, he looked every inch the refined guest, but his sharp blue eyes scanned the crowd with a predator's focus. His gaze paused briefly on the center of the ballroom, where Isaac Fontaine stood surrounded by his entourage. The crime lord's calm demeanor and faint smile masked the deadly power he wielded over everyone present.

In the distance, Irina moved through the crowd with practiced ease, her navy gown flowing like liquid silk as she approached a group of dignitaries. For a brief moment, her sharp green eyes flicked toward Jack before she slipped seamlessly into conversation, her laugh a light, practiced melody.

"Try not to look like you're hunting someone," Irina murmured through her concealed mic.

Jack smirked faintly, brushing the cuff of his jacket to adjust his hidden earpiece. "I thought brooding was part of the charm."

"Your charm needs work," Irina replied dryly.

THE EVENING'S gala was a cover for something far more sinister. Fontaine had organized the event as a meeting ground for The Veil's financial backers—a chance to solidify their plans and ensure the coordinated attacks on Berlin, Paris, and Rome would proceed without interference.

Jack's focus shifted as Markus Herrick, Fontaine's logistics man, entered the room. The man's sharp suit and stony expression made him easy to spot. Herrick's calculated strides and the intensity in his eyes marked him as someone deeply entrenched in Fontaine's schemes.

"He's here," Jack murmured.

"Focus on Herrick," Irina replied. "I'll handle the rest."

Jack's smirk faded as he descended the staircase, blending seamlessly into the crowd.

IRINA'S TASK was far more delicate. Her target wasn't Fontaine or Herrick—it was Maria Ortega, the EISA operative whose shadowy allegiance to The Veil had placed her at the conspiracy's center. Ortega stood near a cluster of European officials, her tailored suit and commanding presence making her impossible to ignore.

Irina approached cautiously, her tone light as she joined the conversation. "Ambassador Delgado," she said, addressing one of the officials, "I've been meaning to discuss your recent trade negotiations. Fascinating work."

Delgado smiled, gesturing for Irina to join them. Ortega's eyes flicked toward her briefly before returning to the conversation, her expression unreadable.

As Irina slipped into the group, her concealed mic transmitted the interaction to Jack. "I'm with Ortega now. She's not leaving without answers."

JACK FOLLOWED Herrick to a secluded corner of the ballroom. The logistics man spoke in low tones with a tall, gray-haired man whose identity was obscured by the dim light. Jack moved closer, his steps silent as he positioned himself within earshot.

"...shipments will move on schedule," Herrick was saying. "Berlin and Paris are secured. Rome requires additional measures, but the assets are in place."

The gray-haired man nodded. "The Veil will handle any complications. Fontaine's role is critical, but it is not irreplaceable."

Jack's jaw tightened as he processed the words. Fontaine, the puppet master, was himself just a pawn—one the Veil was ready to discard.

He moved back into the crowd, his voice low as he addressed Irina. "Herrick just confirmed it. Fontaine's expendable. The Veil's ready to cut him loose if he steps out of line."

"Good," Irina replied. "Then we'll push him to the edge."

IRINA'S CONVERSATION with Ortega turned confrontational as the group of officials dispersed. Maneuvering closer to the EISA operative, she lowered her voice. "Maria, a word?"

Ortega's gaze sharpened, her expression cool. "Irina Stepanov. What an unexpected surprise."

"I could say the same," Irina replied, her voice edged with steel. "You've been busy. The Veil's reach is impressive."

Ortega's lips curved into a faint smile. "Careful, Irina. Accusations like that can be dangerous."

Irina stepped closer, her tone soft but deadly. "Dangerous is leaking intel to criminals. Dangerous is orchestrating attacks that destabilize entire nations. What's your endgame, Maria? Money? Power?"

Ortega's smile faded, replaced by an icy glare. "You're out of your depth, Stepanov. Walk away while you still can."

"I'll take that as a confirmation," Irina said, her green eyes blazing. "But I don't walk away. You should know that by now."

THE NIGHT'S crescendo came when Fontaine himself took the stage to address the room. The crowd quieted as the crime lord's deep voice carried across the ballroom.

"Ladies and gentlemen," Fontaine began, his tone smooth and confident. "Tonight is a celebration of collaboration, a testament to what we can achieve together. Our future is secure because of the partnerships we've built—and the resolve we've shown to protect them."

Jack and Irina exchanged a glance, their shared understanding unspoken. Fontaine's words were calculated to reassure his backers, but the cracks in his network were becoming more visible by the moment.

As applause filled the room, Irina slipped away from Ortega, her steps quick but controlled as she rejoined Jack near the bar.

"Anything useful?" Jack asked.

Irina's expression was unreadable. "Enough to know Ortega won't let this operation fail. She's too invested."

Jack's jaw tightened. "Then we take her down with the rest of them."

THE GALA BEGAN to wind down, but the tension between Jack and Irina remained palpable as they exited the Palais Reinhardt. The brisk night air was a sharp contrast to the ballroom's warmth, their breaths visible as they walked toward their waiting car.

"This changes everything," Irina said quietly, her gaze distant.

Jack glanced at her, his smirk faint. "Not everything. We're still the ones cleaning up their mess."

Irina allowed herself a small smile, though it didn't reach her eyes. "Let's make sure we do it right."

As the car pulled away from Vienna's glittering lights, the enormity of their mission weighed heavily on them. The Veil's plans were clearer than ever, but so were the stakes—and the cost of failure.

CHAPTER 8
COLLATERAL DAMAGE

THE LABORATORY WASN'T MARKED on any map, but Jack and Irina had tracked its location through the stolen shipment manifest and encrypted communications from Fontaine's villa. Tucked deep within an abandoned industrial complex in Eastern Europe, the facility appeared nondescript on the surface—a cluster of weathered warehouses surrounded by overgrown vegetation and a single perimeter fence.

The illusion of neglect ended the moment they slipped through the gates. Armed guards patrolled in tight rotations, their movements precise and professional. Security cameras panned in synchronized sweeps, their lenses gleaming in the dim moonlight.

Jack crouched behind a stack of rusting barrels near the outer wall, his sharp blue eyes scanning the courtyard. "Fontaine isn't messing around," he murmured into his mic. "This isn't just a lab—it's a fortress."

"Fortresses fall," Irina replied softly, her voice calm despite the tension. From her position near the fence, she could see the faint glow of lights spilling from one of the buildings, silhouetting technicians inside.

Jack smirked faintly, adjusting the strap of his tactical vest. "Let's hope you're right. How's our entry point?"

Irina's green eyes flicked to the side door she'd identified during their surveillance. A guard lingered nearby, his rifle slung across his chest as he checked his watch. "Clear in sixty seconds. Don't fall behind."

"Never do," Jack replied.

THE INTERIOR of the facility was cold and sterile, its fluorescent lights casting a harsh glow over rows of gleaming metal tables and equipment. The faint hum of machines filled the air, broken occasionally by the muffled voices of technicians moving between workstations.

Jack and Irina moved silently through the labyrinth of corridors, their footsteps muffled by the rubber soles of their boots. Their goal was clear: the secure storage room deep within the lab, where Fontaine's people had stashed the biochemicals and blueprints critical to The Veil's plan.

"Anything on the cameras?" Jack whispered.

Irina tapped the small tablet she carried, her fingers navigating the hacked security feed. "Two guards in the hallway outside the storage room. I'll handle them. You focus on the lock."

Jack arched an eyebrow. "Handle them how?"

"You'll see," Irina replied, her tone dry.

THE GUARDS never saw her coming. Irina emerged from the shadows, her movements fluid and precise. A swift blow to the first man's temple sent him crumpling silently to the ground. Before the second guard could react, Irina spun, her silenced pistol firing a single, well-placed shot that dropped him instantly.

Jack appeared seconds later, his smirk faint as he knelt beside the lock on the storage room door. "Remind me to never get on your bad side."

Irina didn't reply, her attention already on the hallway.

INSIDE THE STORAGE ROOM, the air was cold, and the faint scent of chemicals lingered. Jack's flashlight illuminated rows of metal shelves, each lined with carefully labeled containers and folders. His sharp gaze swept over the labels, recognizing the components of mass destruction.

"Got it," Jack said, pulling a slim file from one of the shelves. The folder contained blueprints for the attacks, along with a list of operatives assigned to each city.

Irina joined him, her expression hard as she flipped through the pages. "This confirms it. They're hitting water supplies and energy grids. Fontaine's people aren't just enabling the attacks—they're executing them."

Jack nodded grimly, tucking the file into his bag. "Let's move. This place is going to blow in ten."

Irina arched an eyebrow. "You rigged explosives?"

Jack's smirk returned. "Of course I rigged explosives."

THEIR ESCAPE WASN'T CLEAN.

As they exited the storage room, alarms blared, their piercing wail echoing through the facility. Red lights bathed the corridors, and the sound of boots pounding on concrete grew louder.

Jack fired twice, his shots precise as they moved toward the exit. "Guess they noticed we were here."

Irina's voice was sharp. "Less commentary, more shooting."

They ducked behind a row of equipment as gunfire erupted, bullets sparking against the metal. Jack reloaded quickly, his movements smooth despite the chaos.

"Cover me," he said, nodding toward the side door.

Irina leaned out, her silenced pistol firing in controlled bursts as Jack darted toward the exit. He slammed the door open, motioning for her to follow.

THE COURTYARD WAS CHAOS. Guards swarmed the area, their shouts mixing with the roar of engines as vehicles circled the perimeter. Jack and Irina sprinted toward the fence, their breaths visible in the chilly night air.

Jack dropped to one knee, firing at the nearest guard as Irina scaled the fence with practiced ease. She landed lightly on the other side, turning to cover Jack as he followed.

As they disappeared into the darkness, the ground trembled with the force of the explosions. Flames erupted from the facility, casting a fiery glow over the countryside as smoke billowed into the sky.

Jack glanced over his shoulder, his smirk faint. "That should slow them down."

Irina didn't smile, her expression grim as they moved toward their waiting vehicle. "Not enough. Fontaine's people won't stop just because we destroyed a lab. If anything, they'll move faster."

Jack nodded, his smirk fading. "Then so do we."

THE RIDE back to their secondary safe house was silent, the weight of what they'd uncovered pressing heavily on them both.

As Jack parked the car in the shadows of an abandoned farmhouse, he glanced at Irina. "We've got what we need to stop them. But this thing with The Veil? It's bigger than Fontaine."

Irina nodded, her green eyes hard. "It always was. And if we don't stop them here, no one will."

Jack leaned back in his seat, his expression grim. "Then let's make sure we finish this."

After a pause, Jack asked, his voice quieter, "What happens when The Veil's gone? Do we just go back to the way things were?"

Irina's green eyes locked onto his. "There's no going back, Jack. Not for people like us."

Jack hesitated, his jaw tightening. "You sure about that? Because sometimes it feels like you're fighting your own battle—and I'm just along for the ride."

Irina's voice softened, though her gaze remained sharp. "Trust goes both ways, Jones. If you think I've got a secret agenda, maybe you should say so."

The silence between them was heavy, broken only by the faint hum of the car's heater. Finally, Jack exhaled, his tension easing slightly. "We finish this. Then we figure out the rest."

CHAPTER 9
BREAKING POINT

THE ABANDONED military outpost stood as a relic of a bygone era, its crumbling concrete walls and rusting guard towers hidden deep within the Balkan mountains. The narrow dirt road leading to the site had been overgrown with weeds, and the cold wind carried the faint scent of pine and decay.

Jack Jones crouched behind a jagged boulder at the edge of the outpost, his sharp blue eyes scanning the perimeter. Armed guards patrolled in pairs, their breath visible in the cold night air. Floodlights illuminated the main building, casting harsh shadows across the cracked asphalt.

"Lovely place," Jack murmured into his concealed mic. "Fontaine sure knows how to pick his hideouts."

From her position on a ridge overlooking the site, Irina Stepanov's voice came through softly. "Don't get comfortable. Karpov's here. This isn't a retreat—it's his last stand."

Jack smirked faintly. "Then let's make it count."

THE PLAN WAS simple in theory: Jack would infiltrate the outpost, retrieve the intel Fontaine's lieutenant, Anton Karpov, had on the biochem shipments, and extract before reinforcements could arrive. Irina would provide overwatch, her sniper rifle ready to eliminate threats.

As Jack moved toward the outpost, his instincts buzzed with unease. Karpov wasn't the type to leave loose ends, and the increased security suggested he wasn't just hiding—he was preparing for a fight.

Jack slipped through a gap in the perimeter fence, his movements silent as he avoided the floodlights. The guards were disciplined, their patrol patterns tight, but Jack's years of fieldwork had honed his ability to move unseen.

"I'm in," Jack whispered.

"Main building," Irina replied. "Third floor. Karpov's holed up in a command room. Expect resistance."

Jack nodded, his grip tightening on his pistol. "Wouldn't want it any other way."

INSIDE THE MAIN BUILDING, the air was heavy with the scent of oil and mildew. The faint hum of a generator echoed through the narrow hallways, and Jack's footsteps were barely audible over the sound.

He climbed the staircase carefully, his senses sharp as he reached the third floor. The command room was at the end of the hall, its door guarded by two men armed with assault rifles.

"Two guards outside the room," Jack murmured.

"On my mark," Irina replied.

Jack counted the seconds as the faint crack of Irina's rifle echoed through his earpiece. The first guard crumpled to the ground, a precise shot to the head dropping him instantly. Before the second guard could react, Jack surged forward, his pistol silenced as he took the man down with a single shot.

"Clean work," Irina said.

"Always," Jack replied, pushing open the command room door.

KARPOV WAS WAITING.

The lieutenant stood behind a metal table littered with maps and documents, his pale blue eyes cold and calculating. He held a pistol in one hand, the other resting on the edge of the table.

"Jones," Karpov said, his tone sharp. "I was wondering when you'd show up."

Jack stepped inside, his own pistol raised. "Looks like I'm right on time."

Karpov smirked faintly, his gaze flicking to the documents on the table. "You've been a thorn in Fontaine's side for far too long. But this? This is where it ends."

Jack's voice was steely. "Funny. I was about to say the same thing."

THE ROOM ERUPTED into chaos as Karpov opened fire, his shots ringing out in the confined space. Jack dove behind a heavy metal cabinet, bullets ricocheting and sending sparks flying.

"Karpov's putting up a fight," Jack muttered into his mic.

"Stay alive," Irina replied. "I'm on my way."

Jack rolled out from cover, firing twice. One shot grazed Karpov's shoulder, drawing a sharp hiss of pain from the lieutenant. The second struck the edge of the table, scattering papers across the floor.

Karpov snarled, his voice cutting through the gunfire. "You think you can stop this? Fontaine's already won. The Veil's plan is unstoppable."

Jack moved closer, his steps quick and precise. "Maybe, but you won't be around to see it."

The fight was brutal, a close-quarters clash of precision and raw determination. Jack's training and reflexes gave him the edge, but Karpov's desperation made him dangerous.

Jack managed to knock the pistol from Karpov's hand, sending it skidding across the floor. Karpov lunged for it, but Jack tackled him, slamming him against the wall.

Karpov gasped for breath, his cold eyes blazing with fury. "You think taking me down will change anything?"

"It's a start," Jack replied, driving his fist into Karpov's jaw. The lieutenant crumpled to the ground, unconscious.

IRINA ARRIVED MOMENTS LATER, her silenced pistol raised as she scanned the room. Her sharp green eyes landed on Karpov's prone form, then shifted to Jack.

"You're bleeding," she said, nodding to the shallow graze on his arm.

"Just a scratch," Jack replied, his smirk faint. "Karpov's a talker. Let's see what he knows."

They moved quickly, gathering the documents from the table and securing Karpov with zip ties. The files confirmed their fears: Fontaine's shipments were en route, and The Veil's attacks on Berlin, Paris, and Rome were imminent.

"This is it," Irina said quietly, her voice edged with determination. "We have everything we need to stop them."

Jack nodded, his expression grim. "Then let's make it count."

As THEY EXITED THE OUTPOST, the faint hum of approaching engines sent a chill down Jack's spine.

"Reinforcements," he muttered.

Irina's voice was sharp. "We're out of time."

They sprinted toward the tree line, their movements quick and precise as the sound of gunfire erupted behind them. Jack fired twice over his shoulder, his shots forcing their pursuers to take cover.

They reached their waiting vehicle moments later, Jack gunning the engine as Irina scanned the rearview mirror for signs of pursuit.

"We've got what we came for," Irina said, her tone steady.

Jack's smirk returned, though it was faint. "Now we just have to stay alive long enough to use it."

The night stretched on as they drove into the mountains, the enormity of their mission weighing heavily on them both. Fontaine's network was crumbling, but The Veil's plan was still in motion—and their fight was far from over.

CHAPTER 10
INTO THE SHADOWS

THE CITY of Zurich sparkled below, a dazzling mix of historic spires and modern high-rises against the inky backdrop of the Swiss night. From their perch on a wooded ridge, Jack Jones and Irina Stepanov studied the estate nestled in the forest on the outskirts of the city. Its modernist architecture—a stark fusion of steel and glass—contrasted sharply with the wilderness surrounding it. The estate's walls glowed faintly under floodlights, casting long shadows over the compound's manicured lawns.

Jack adjusted his binoculars, his sharp blue eyes scanning the perimeter. Armed guards moved in tight patrols, their rifles slung but ready. A high-tech security system linked the estate's cameras and motion sensors, creating an almost impenetrable barrier of surveillance.

"Fontaine's last stand," Jack murmured, lowering the binoculars.

Irina stood beside him, her breath visible in the frigid air. She wore a black tactical jacket over sleek combat gear, her green eyes sharp as they swept the compound. "And he's not going down without a fight. The Veil's sending their best to make sure this shipment leaves on time."

Jack smirked faintly, his tone dry. "Guess we'd better disappoint them."

THE INFILTRATION BEGAN with deliberate precision. Jack and Irina moved through the dense underbrush like shadows, their boots crunching softly on the frost-laden ground. The forest around them was eerily quiet, the wind rustling the bare branches as if holding its breath.

Ahead, the estate loomed, its sleek glass walls reflecting the glow of the city in the distance. The guards' movements were methodical, their rotations leaving little margin for error.

"East entrance," Irina whispered into her mic, nodding toward a side door partially obscured by a low hedge. "Two guards. Cameras looped."

The estate's modernist design proved deceptive. Once inside, Jack and Irina found themselves navigating a maze of reflective glass walls and seamless steel doors. Every step they took seemed amplified in the sterile stillness, the sound ricocheting in unnatural ways.

"Something's off," Irina murmured.

Jack nodded, his blue eyes narrowing. "Acoustics aren't right. It's a sound trap—every move we make is being recorded and analyzed."

Ahead, a red laser beam flickered to life, scanning the hallway. Jack grabbed Irina's arm, pulling her back.

"Infrared grid," he muttered. "They're not just expecting company —they're hunting it."

Irina glanced at the floor-to-ceiling windows lining the corridor. Her lips curved into a faint smile as she pulled a grappling hook from her pack. "Then we don't give them the satisfaction. How's your climbing, Jones?"

THE COMMAND CENTER was exactly as Jack had expected: a sleek, high-tech nerve hub with walls of glowing monitors and maps. Live feeds displayed the movement of shipments across Europe, while countdowns ticked ominously beneath the names of targeted cities—Berlin, Paris, Rome.

Jack approached the central console, his fingers flying over the keyboard. "I'll pull the intel and set a kill switch for the entire system. We take this offline, and Fontaine's network collapses."

Irina covered the doorway, her silenced pistol at the ready. "Make it fast. Reinforcements are coming."

The sound of heavy boots echoed down the hall as the first wave of guards approached. Irina fired in controlled bursts, her shots precise and lethal.

"Company," she said sharply.

Jack didn't look up. "I noticed."

The guards were relentless, their shouts echoing through the estate as they attempted to breach the command center. Irina moved like a ghost, her pistol firing with surgical accuracy. Jack remained focused, his expression grim as he bypassed firewalls and initiated the shutdown sequence.

"Got it," Jack said finally, yanking a portable drive from the console. "All the data's here—routes, operatives, everything."

"Good," Irina replied. "Now let's get out before we're cornered."

***

THEIR ESCAPE TOOK them back through the estate, the once-quiet halls now alive with chaos. Alarms blared, and the glow of emergency lights bathed everything in red.

In the main atrium, Fontaine waited.

The crime lord stood at the base of the grand staircase, his sharp suit smeared with blood. He held a pistol in one hand, his dark eyes blazing with fury as they locked onto Jack and Irina.

"You think you've won?" Fontaine snarled, his voice echoing. "The Veil doesn't need me to finish this. They'll come for you. They'll burn your world to ash."

Jack stepped forward, his own pistol raised. "Let them try. But you won't be around to see it."

Fontaine's smirk was bitter. "Neither will you."

The standoff ended in a heartbeat. Fontaine's hand twitched toward his trigger, but Jack fired first. The shot was clean and precise, striking Fontaine squarely in the chest. The crime lord staggered, his pistol falling from his grasp as he collapsed onto the marble floor.

Jack lowered his weapon, his expression unreadable as he turned to Irina. "Let's go."

THEIR FINAL SPRINT through the estate was a blur of gunfire and flashing lights. Irina led the way, her movements quick and deliberate as she cleared a path to the perimeter. Jack followed close behind, his focus sharp despite the chaos.

By the time they reached the tree line, the estate was in flames, the explosion of Jack's planted charges lighting up the night sky.

"Nice touch," Irina said, glancing at the inferno.

Jack smirked faintly. "Thought it'd make a statement."

AS THEY DROVE AWAY from Zurich, the weight of their victory hung heavily between them. Fontaine's network was dismantled, but The Veil's shadow loomed larger than ever.

Irina leaned back in her seat, her green eyes distant. "We've hit them hard. But it's not enough."

Jack nodded, his hands gripping the wheel. "Then we keep going. No more shadows. No more half-measures."

Irina's faint smile held no humor. "Together?"

Jack's smirk returned, though it was tinged with exhaustion. "Always."

IN A DIMLY LIT office halfway across the world, the remaining members of The Veil's inner council sat around a circular table. The room was silent save for the faint hum of a projector displaying a map of Europe.

"Fontaine has failed," one of them said, his voice cold. "But his network is intact. For now."

A woman in a tailored suit leaned forward, her expression unreadable. "Failure was inevitable. What matters is how we adapt."

"The operatives in Berlin and Paris are ready," another voice added. "Phase Two proceeds on schedule."

The first speaker nodded. "Then let's ensure our friends in Zurich understand that Fontaine's mistakes won't be tolerated."

The End

ENDGAME

A SHORT THRILLER

CHAPTER 1
UNRAVELING THE WEB

ZURICH AT NIGHT was a city of contradictions. Its cobblestone streets and centuries-old facades exuded an air of timeless sophistication, but behind the gleaming glass towers of its financial district, secrets thrived. For Jack Jones and Irina Stepanov, it was a battlefield cloaked in wealth and civility.

The duo crouched in the shadow of a delivery truck parked in a dimly lit alley. The distant hum of traffic masked their whispered conversation, and the crisp night air stung their exposed skin. Neither seemed to notice, their attention locked on the office building ahead—a monolith of steel and glass that towered over the skyline like a sentinel.

"This is where the money flows," Irina murmured, her voice barely audible against the wind. "If Fontaine's network had a heartbeat, it ran through here. Now The Veil's taken over the controls."

Jack adjusted the strap on his tactical vest, his sharp blue eyes sweeping the building's mirrored façade. Guards patrolled the entrance in disciplined formations, their nondescript uniforms and efficient movements betraying their elite training. "And if we're right, this is where we find out how deep The Veil's roots go."

Irina smirked faintly, though her green eyes stayed hard. "Always fun to crash a party uninvited."

Jack glanced at her, a dry humor glinting in his gaze. "Let's make sure they don't forget us."

THE INFILTRATION BEGAN IN SILENCE. Jack and Irina moved as one, slipping through a side entrance they'd scouted during the day. The service corridor inside smelled of industrial grease and faintly acrid cleaning chemicals, its sterile white walls devoid of personality.

Irina pulled up a schematic of the building on her tablet, the blueprints glowing softly in the dim hallway. Her fingers darted across the screen with practiced ease. "Data servers are on the fifteenth floor. That's where we'll find the transfer logs and payouts—the financial threads tying The Veil together."

Jack nodded, checking his silenced pistol. "And the security office?"

"Two floors up," she replied, her tone brisk. "We'll have to pass it on the way down. Expect company."

"Good," Jack muttered, his lips curving into a faint smile. "It's been too quiet lately."

THE ELEVATOR HUMMED SOFTLY as it carried them upward, its polished interior reflecting their tense expressions. The weight of their mission pressed heavily in the confined space, the quiet hum amplifying every heartbeat.

When the doors slid open on the fifteenth floor, the sterile, open-plan office stretched out before them. Rows of sleek desks and glowing monitors gave the space a clinical efficiency, while the faint hum of machinery emanated from the server room at the far end.

"This place feels wrong," Jack murmured, his sharp gaze scanning the room.

Irina smirked faintly. "The Veil's not sloppy. Precision is their trademark."

The server room door required a keycard, but Irina's tools made quick work of the lock. Inside, the air was cold, heavy with the whirring of hard drives. Irina moved quickly, connecting her tablet to the network terminal.

"Logs are transferring now," she said, her voice calm but deliberate. "This will give us everything—payouts, shell companies, offshore accounts. We'll know who's funding The Veil and how they're moving the money."

Jack positioned himself by the door, his pistol raised and ready. "Make it quick. I don't like staying in one place for too long."

THE FIRST SIGN of trouble came as muffled voices drifted down the hallway. Jack's ears picked up the distinct rhythm of boots on tile, accompanied by the metallic clink of weapons being readied.

"Company," he muttered, his voice low.

Irina didn't look up. "Two minutes."

Jack's smirk was faint as his pistol rose, aimed at the door. When the handle began to turn, he fired. The first guard fell before he could react, the suppressed shot barely a whisper in the still air. The second hesitated, his hesitation costing him as Jack closed the distance, slamming the man against the wall with ruthless efficiency.

"Two minutes," Jack repeated, kicking the unconscious guard's weapon aside.

Irina's fingers moved in a blur, her eyes locked on the screen. The tablet chimed softly. "Done. Every account, every transfer. The Veil's web is mapped out."

"Then we're done here," Jack said, pulling her toward the door.

THEIR ESCAPE WAS anything but quiet. By the time they reached the thirteenth floor, the building was alive with alarms. Red emergency lights pulsed in rhythmic bursts, casting jagged shadows along the walls.

Jack moved with precision, firing at the guards who swarmed

toward them. His shots were calculated, each one aimed to incapacitate without excessive force.

"Elevators are out," Irina said sharply, her gaze snapping toward a glowing exit sign. "Stairs to the left."

Jack nodded, reloading as they pushed through a pair of double doors into the stairwell. Footsteps echoed above and below, the sharp staccato of pursuit. Jack's sharp gaze caught a maintenance hatch overhead, its edges outlined in dust.

"This way," he said, motioning for Irina to follow as he boosted her up.

The maintenance ducts were tight and dusty, their narrow metal passages forcing them to move in silence. The faint voices of guards below added to the tension, but Jack and Irina pressed on, finally emerging into a dimly lit parking garage beneath the building.

THEIR GETAWAY CAR—A nondescript sedan with tinted windows— waited in the shadows. Jack slid into the driver's seat, the engine purring softly as he maneuvered out onto the deserted street.

Irina sat beside him, her tablet still glowing with the stolen data. "This isn't just offshore accounts and shell companies," she said, her voice edged with urgency. "These payouts are tied to sitting politicians, corporate executives, even intelligence officials. The Veil's not infiltrating power—they've already done it."

Jack's jaw tightened, his grip on the wheel firm. "And no one's noticed—or cared."

Irina's green eyes locked on his. "We notice. That's enough."

Jack smirked faintly, though his expression stayed grim. "Let's hope so."

As the glittering lights of Zurich faded in the rearview mirror, the weight of their discovery settled over them. They'd uncovered The Veil's financial lifeline, but exposing it would come at a price.

The road ahead was darker than ever.

And allies were running out.

CHAPTER 2
FRIENDS OR FOES

THE MORNING RAIN swept across London in relentless waves, a gray veil that blurred the city's iconic skyline. Jack Jones and Irina Stepanov sat silently in the back of a black cab weaving through narrow streets. Their destination loomed ahead—a nondescript building tucked between rows of Georgian facades. The polished brass plate near the entrance read: **NESA Headquarters.**

Jack adjusted the collar of his coat, his sharp blue eyes scanning the rain-slicked street for signs of trouble. "Feels strange coming back here. Like walking into a trap."

Irina smirked faintly, though her green eyes flicked across the windows with equal vigilance. "It's only a trap if you're not ready for it. You brought your charm, right?"

Jack snorted softly, his voice edged with dry humor. "Charm won't mean much when they've got guns pointed at us."

"Then I hope you brought something sharper," Irina replied, her tone cool.

THE RECEPTION AREA inside NESA Headquarters was sterile, all polished floors and muted lighting. The hum of quiet conversations mixed with the faint clatter of keyboards, creating an illusion of calm. Jack and Irina strode through the space with the assurance of seasoned operatives, though both felt the weight of unspoken tension pressing against them.

Jack caught the subtle, wary glances of passing agents, their whispers poorly masked. Irina's sharp gaze tracked the faint shifts in security personnel—guards discreetly repositioning to block exits, their movements deliberate.

"Definitely a trap," Jack murmured under his breath.

"Stay calm," Irina replied softly, her expression unreadable. "We need them to listen before they decide to shoot."

DIRECTOR MARTIN HADLEY was waiting for them in his office, seated behind a heavy oak desk that dominated the room. The space was windowless, its neutral decor offering no distraction from the man himself. Hadley's steely gray eyes locked onto Jack and Irina as they entered, his presence radiating authority.

"You've got nerve showing up here," Hadley said, his voice as sharp as a scalpel. "The last time we spoke, you were being disavowed."

Jack smirked faintly, taking a seat without waiting for an invitation. "Disavowed, framed—same thing these days. We're here because you need to hear what we've found."

Hadley's gaze shifted to Irina, his expression hard to read. "And you? Still playing both sides?"

Irina's lips curved into a faint smile that didn't reach her eyes. "I play the only side that matters—stopping The Veil."

Hadley leaned back in his chair, folding his hands with deliberate slowness. "And why should I believe anything you say?"

Jack pulled a portable drive from his coat pocket, placing it on the desk with a quiet click. "Because this doesn't lie. Financial records, transfer logs, payouts—all tied to The Veil's operations. Their network runs deeper than you think, and it's active in places you wouldn't expect."

Hadley stared at the drive for a long moment, his sharp gaze unyielding. Finally, he picked it up, turning it over in his hands. "If this is legitimate, it's the kind of intel that could dismantle The Veil's entire operation."

"That's the idea," Irina said coolly. "But we can't do it alone. We need resources, contacts—"

Hadley's sharp laugh interrupted her. "You've got nerve asking for help after going rogue. You're fugitives, and most of this agency would rather see you dead than shake your hand."

Jack's smirk disappeared, his tone hardening. "So you'd rather protect your reputation than stop a group that's about to destabilize half of Europe?"

Hadley's eyes narrowed, his voice dropping a degree colder. "You think you're the only ones trying to stop them? This agency has protocols, chains of command. We don't act on the whims of two ex-operatives trying to clear their names."

Irina leaned forward, her voice cutting through the tension like a blade. "While you're busy following protocols, The Veil is orchestrating attacks that will collapse entire governments. Your bureaucracy won't stop them—but we can."

Hadley stood abruptly, his jaw tightening. "You've made your point. I'll review the intel, but don't expect favors. And don't think for a second you're welcome here."

THE TENSION in the office clung to them like smoke as Jack and Irina exited. The sterile hallways seemed narrower, the agents' stares sharper and more scrutinizing. Jack's instincts buzzed with warning as he noticed subtle shifts in posture from the guards near the exit.

"Something's off," Jack murmured, his voice low.

Irina's green eyes swept the room with practiced precision. "They're stalling us."

The echo of boots behind them was all the confirmation they needed. Jack turned, his hand inching toward his weapon as a team of armed agents closed in.

"Jones. Stepanov," the lead agent barked. "You're coming with us."

Jack's smirk returned, though it was tinged with irritation. "Not likely."

Before the words finished leaving his mouth, Irina moved. Her elbow struck the agent's wrist, sending his weapon clattering to the floor. Jack followed with a sharp kick to the next guard, disarming him in one fluid motion.

The hallway exploded into chaos, but Jack and Irina moved with precision born of experience. Years of training transformed the confined space into an advantage as they neutralized the agents, leaving a trail of groaning bodies in their wake.

THE RAIN HAD INTENSIFIED by the time they slipped out onto the crowded streets of London. Umbrellas and hurried footsteps blurred around them, providing perfect cover as they blended into the throng.

Jack's coat was damp, his sharp blue eyes scanning for any signs of pursuit. "Well, that went about as well as expected," he muttered, his tone dripping with sarcasm.

Irina smirked faintly, though her voice was serious. "Safe to say NESA's not going to be an ally."

Jack's jaw tightened, his expression grim. "No. But they just confirmed one thing."

Irina glanced at him, her sharp gaze narrowing. "What's that?"

Jack's tone was low, his voice edged with steel. "The Veil's reach is deeper than we thought. And we're on our own."

CHAPTER 3
THE MASTERMIND'S REACH

THE SOUTH of France was a picture of idyllic beauty—rolling vineyards, sun-drenched cliffs, and the endless azure of the Mediterranean. Yet for Jack Jones and Irina Stepanov, the region's charm was a fragile mask hiding the deadly stakes of their mission.

They crouched at the edge of a sprawling coastal estate, its high walls and guarded perimeter a testament to its owner's paranoia. Beyond the barriers lay an opulent fortress, its pale stone façade glowing faintly in the soft evening light.

"Fontaine would've killed for a place like this," Jack muttered, adjusting the strap of his tactical bag.

Irina smirked faintly, her green eyes locked on the estate through her binoculars. "Except he didn't have the clout to host a gathering like this. Volkov's the real deal—a diplomat who moonlights as a criminal mastermind."

"Or a criminal mastermind who moonlights as a diplomat," Jack replied, his tone dry.

The estate buzzed with activity. Sleek luxury cars lined the circular driveway, their polished black exteriors gleaming under floodlights. Guests in tailored suits and flowing gowns moved toward the grand entrance, their elegance disguising the dangerous deals being struck within.

Lowering her binoculars, Irina's expression hardened. "This isn't just a social call. Volkov's consolidating power—brokering alliances to tighten The Veil's grip on Europe."

Jack's smirk deepened slightly. "Then let's give them something to talk about."

THE PLAN WAS DECEPTIVELY SIMPLE: infiltrate the gathering under assumed identities, gather intel on Volkov's operations, and leave without anyone noticing.

Jack adjusted his tie as they approached the estate's grand entrance, his tailored suit immaculate and a far cry from the tactical gear he'd worn just hours earlier. Beside him, Irina exuded confidence, her navy evening gown hugging her frame and moving like liquid silk.

"You clean up well," Jack murmured, his tone light.

Irina arched an eyebrow, her smirk faint. "So do you. Try not to ruin it."

At the door, a stoic guard examined their forged invitations, his sharp eyes lingering on Jack for a beat too long. Jack returned his gaze with a faint smile, his posture relaxed despite the tension coiling beneath his calm exterior.

"Everything in order?" Jack asked, his voice easy.

The guard grunted, handing back the invitations. "Welcome to the estate."

INSIDE, the mansion was a masterclass in opulence. Crystal chandeliers hung from vaulted ceilings, their glow reflecting off marble floors and gilded walls. Guests mingled in the grand ballroom, their laughter and clinking glasses a polished veneer over the undercurrent of tense conversations.

Jack's sharp blue eyes swept the room, cataloging the positions of security personnel stationed at discreet but strategic points. He moved fluidly through the crowd, his every step measured.

Irina drifted away with equal precision, her movements unhurried as she approached a cluster of diplomats deep in discussion. Through Jack's concealed earpiece, her voice came softly: "Volkov's in the study. Looks like he's holding court."

Jack adjusted his cufflinks, his tone casual. "Guess I'll mingle while you make an impression."

VOLKOV WAS everything Jack had expected: tall and silver-haired, with the quiet gravitas of a man who wielded power as easily as others drew breath. He stood at the head of a long table in the study, his sharp suit impeccably tailored. Around him, men and women in dark suits listened intently, their postures deferential.

"This operation is not about chaos," Volkov said, his faint Eastern European accent underscoring the weight of his words. "It is about control. With infrastructure in disarray, we will shape the world to our liking."

Jack lingered near the shadows of the study's entrance, blending into the muted lighting. His sharp ears caught fragments of the conversation—energy grids, financial institutions, strategic assets—all threads in a larger plan.

"They're not just planning attacks," Jack murmured into his mic. "They're planning reconstruction on their terms. Control the aftermath, and they control everything."

Irina's reply was crisp. "Focus on the target. We need names, locations, anything actionable."

WHILE JACK GATHERED intel in the shadows, Irina worked the ballroom with equal efficiency. Her sharp wit and poised demeanor made her an instant magnet for the diplomats, eager to share their opinions and, unwittingly, their secrets.

Her target was a nervous young aide who had consumed one too many glasses of champagne. Irina leaned closer, her tone light yet inquisitive, her green eyes locking onto his.

"You're close to Volkov, aren't you?" she asked, her smile faint but inviting.

The aide flushed, his confidence faltering. "I... I assist him, yes."

Irina tilted her head, her interest seemingly casual. "Then you must know what he's planning. I hear rumors about an ambitious energy strategy."

The aide hesitated, his gaze darting around the room as if searching for an escape. "It's not just energy. Volkov is coordinating... broader efforts. But it's not my place to say more."

"You've already said enough," Irina replied smoothly, her tone soft but firm. "Enjoy the party."

***

THE EVENING TOOK a sharp turn when one of Volkov's men noticed Jack lingering near the study. The guard's sharp gaze locked onto him, his hand shifting toward a concealed weapon.

Jack moved first. With a fluid step, he intercepted the guard, his faint smirk masking his readiness. "Lost, friend?"

The guard's curt reply came with a subtle nod toward the study. "You don't belong here."

Before the man could act, Jack struck. His fist connected with the guard's throat, a precise blow that left him gasping and crumpling to the floor. Jack dragged the unconscious man into a nearby alcove, hiding him from view.

"I think my welcome's wearing thin," Jack muttered into his mic.

Irina's voice was sharp. "Then finish up and meet me outside. The ballroom's heating up too."

***

THEY REGROUPED at the estate's perimeter, their polished appearances slightly worse for wear—Irina's gown scuffed at the hem, Jack's tie loosened from the scramble to escape unnoticed.

Jack tossed a stolen folder onto the passenger seat of their waiting car, his smirk faint but triumphant. "Volkov's got big plans, but he's overextending. We've got enough to hit his next move before it launches."

Irina slid into the passenger seat, her green eyes hardened by determination. "He's coordinated, but stretched thin. We take him down at the right moment, and The Veil's entire structure collapses with him."

Jack started the engine, the car rolling smoothly away from the estate. "Then let's make sure we're there for the collapse."

As the glowing mansion disappeared in the rearview mirror, the enormity of their mission pressed heavily on them. The Veil's reach was wider than they'd imagined, but for the first time, their target felt tangible.

And the stakes had never been higher.

CHAPTER 4
COMPROMISED
LOYALTIES

BERLIN'S SKYLINE loomed gray and solemn under a heavy sky, the threat of rain pressing down like a weight. The safe house, hidden in the industrial outskirts of the city, was as unassuming as it was temporary. Cracked walls, dim lighting, and sparse furniture spoke to the urgency of Jack and Irina's operation—a far cry from the opulent settings they'd navigated just days before.

Jack paced the room, restless energy crackling in his movements. On the battered table beside him, a laptop displayed a digital map, Volkov's network of operatives marked with pins that stretched across Europe like a sinister web.

"They're everywhere," Jack muttered, raking a hand through his hair. "Paris, Rome, Berlin... even London. Volkov's people aren't just executing the attacks—they're embedding themselves in the aftermath. Media control, puppet governments, financial reconstruction. They've planned for every contingency."

Irina sat across from him, her sharp green eyes focused on the screen. "That's what makes them dangerous. They're not just tearing systems apart—they're building their own world on the rubble."

Jack's gaze snapped to her, his voice hard. "And what about the people helping them? The ones on our side of the fence?"

Irina didn't flinch. "That's why we're here. To expose them before it's too late."

The air in the room grew heavier as Jack leaned over the table, his blue eyes narrowing. "We can't do this alone. We need allies—someone with the reach to act on this intel before the next attack hits."

"And who exactly do you trust with that?" Irina asked, her tone edged with skepticism. "Hadley? The man who sent a kill team after us in London?"

Jack's jaw tightened, the memory of the ambush still fresh. "Not him. But there's someone else."

Irina frowned. "Who?"

"Duncan Gray," Jack replied, his tone steady. "An analyst. Old school, doesn't play politics. If anyone can act on this without selling us out, it's him."

Irina's green eyes narrowed, suspicion flickering in her expression. "And if you're wrong?"

Jack smirked faintly. "Then we'll know soon enough."

CONTACTING DUNCAN GRAY meant treading carefully. They arranged a meeting through an encrypted channel, settling on a quiet café near Alexanderplatz. Gray was waiting when they arrived, a wiry man in his late fifties whose thick glasses and graying hair gave him the appearance of an unassuming bureaucrat. But his sharp gaze and deliberate movements revealed the seasoned analyst beneath the exterior.

"You've put me in a tight spot, Jones," Gray said quietly, his voice low as he stirred his coffee. "Associating with you two isn't exactly a career boost."

"Not here to help your career, Duncan," Jack replied, his tone sharp but calm. "We need someone who cares more about stopping The Veil than about office politics."

Gray's gaze shifted to Irina, studying her with professional curiosity. "And you? Still playing spymaster, or are you freelancing these days?"

Irina met his gaze unflinchingly. "I'm with the mission. That's all that matters."

After a moment of silence, Gray nodded. "All right. Show me what you've got."

Jack slid a portable drive across the table, his tone urgent. "Names, locations, transfer records—the whole financial network. This is The Veil's blueprint."

Gray inserted the drive into his tablet, his eyes narrowing as he scanned the data. His expression darkened, the faint lines on his face deepening. "This is... worse than I thought. They're not just creating chaos—they're planning coups. Multiple, coordinated coups."

"That's why we need action," Jack said, leaning forward. "Not reports. Not red tape. Action."

Gray sat back, his hand resting on the table as he considered the enormity of the information. "I can leak this to the right people, but it'll take time. Even then, we're kicking a hornet's nest. The Veil has people everywhere—NESA, EISA, local governments. They'll try to bury this."

"Let them try," Irina said coldly, her tone razor-sharp. "We'll make it impossible."

THEIR ALLIANCE with Gray proved fleeting. Less than an hour after leaving the café, they returned to the safe house to find the door ajar, the faint metallic tang of gunpowder in the air.

"Stay close," Jack muttered, drawing his pistol as he entered cautiously.

The room was a wreck—papers scattered, the laptop smashed, and the faint outline of a struggle etched into the disarray. On the floor lay Gray, unconscious and bleeding from a gash on his temple.

"He's alive," Irina said after checking his pulse, her voice tight with controlled urgency. "Barely."

Jack's jaw clenched as he scanned the room, his sharp eyes catching every detail. "They knew we'd be here. Someone tipped them off."

Irina's expression darkened, her green eyes flashing. "Or Gray wasn't as clean as you thought."

Jack shook his head and pointed to the far wall. A symbol had been scrawled hastily in blood-red paint: a serpent coiled around a globe—the unmistakable mark of The Veil.

"They wanted us to see this," Jack said grimly. "They're sending a message."

Irina's lips pressed into a thin line. "Message received. Let's send one back."

As they prepared to leave, Gray stirred weakly, his voice barely above a whisper. "They... they're watching everything. Your agencies... compromised. Can't... trust anyone."

Jack crouched beside him, urgency burning in his voice. "What else do you know? Where's Volkov's next move?"

Gray's trembling hand gestured toward the shattered laptop. "Paris... biochem... soon."

His words faded as he lost consciousness again, his breathing shallow but steady.

Irina grabbed Jack's arm, her voice sharp. "We need to move. Now."

Jack nodded, his expression hardening as he rose to his feet. "Paris it is."

The city lights of Berlin faded into the distance as their stolen car sped toward the border. The weight of Gray's warning hung heavy in the silence between them, the faint hum of the engine the only sound.

"They're everywhere," Jack said finally, his voice low but simmering with frustration.

Irina's gaze stayed fixed on the road ahead, her voice cool but resolute. "Then we burn them out."

Jack smirked faintly, though no humor touched his eyes. "Together?"

Irina's lips curved into a faint smile, her green eyes glinting with determination. "Always."

The car roared into the night, carrying them toward their next battlefield—and a fight that promised to test the limits of their resolve.

CHAPTER 5
CROSSING LINES

THE PRAGUE SKYLINE was a study in contrasts. Gothic spires jutted into the night sky, their weathered facades bathed in the warm glow of streetlights, while the industrial outskirts cast hard-edged shadows under the harsh glare of fluorescent lights. Jack Jones and Irina Stepanov moved through a labyrinth of narrow alleyways, their footsteps muffled on the rain-slicked pavement, their every step deliberate.

Their destination wasn't marked on any map. The black-market arms bazaar existed only in whispers—a transient haven for mercenaries, smugglers, and opportunists trading tools of destruction. Tonight, it was their stage for dismantling The Veil's next move.

"This place reeks of bad decisions," Jack muttered, his sharp blue eyes scanning the looming warehouse ahead.

Irina smirked faintly, adjusting the neckline of her dark leather jacket to better conceal the compact pistol holstered beneath. "Perfect for us, then."

Jack's smirk was dry but genuine. "Let's hope they buy our story."

Irina's green eyes hardened, her tone dropping. "They will. And if they don't, they won't live long enough to question it."

INSIDE, the warehouse buzzed with tension. Rough wooden tables groaned under the weight of weapons, crates, and ammunition, each stamped with the marks of manufacturers from across the globe. The air was thick with the acrid smell of oil and gunpowder, mingling with the low hum of voices and the occasional sharp laugh.

The crowd was a volatile mix of hardened mercenaries, shadowy brokers, and desperate buyers, each negotiation edged with the unspoken threat of violence. Jack and Irina navigated the chaos with unshakable poise. Jack's dark suit and open collar exuded the easy confidence of a man used to cutting deals, while Irina's sleek black ensemble and razor-sharp gaze warned against testing her patience.

A heavyset man approached, his expression suspicious. "Don't recognize you. New buyers?"

"New but serious," Jack replied smoothly, his voice firm yet casual, laced with authority. "We're looking for something big. Discreet. Non-negotiable."

The man's eyes narrowed as he studied them. "We don't deal with amateurs."

Irina stepped forward, her tone glacial. "And we don't waste time with people who can't deliver."

For a moment, the air between them crackled with unspoken tension. Then the man smirked, jerking his head toward the far end of the warehouse. "Follow me."

THE PRIVATE SECTION of the warehouse was quieter, but the atmosphere was no less charged. Here, deals of far greater magnitude were conducted, hidden from prying eyes. At the center of the space, a long table was strewn with blueprints, tactical maps, and grainy surveillance photos.

Standing over the table was a man Jack recognized instantly: a Veil operative from Zurich, his sharp features and calculating gaze unmistakable.

"New buyers?" the operative asked, his tone clipped and skeptical.

Jack stepped forward, his smirk faint but confident. "New, yes. But very interested. Word is, you've got something that could change the game."

The operative's eyes sharpened, his posture shifting slightly. "And who exactly are you?"

"Let's just say we're in the market for solutions," Jack replied, his voice calm but edged with intent.

The operative studied Jack for a moment, his expression inscrutable, before gesturing to the table. "What you're looking at is... transformative. Compact delivery systems, untraceable payloads. Perfect for targeting infrastructure without drawing too much attention."

Irina's green eyes flicked to the blueprints. Her voice remained cool, but her pulse quickened. The diagrams depicted portable biochem dispersal units, small enough to fit into a suitcase but capable of devastating water supplies, air systems, or transportation hubs.

"Impressive," Irina said evenly. "But what about Paris? Word is they're getting something special."

The operative's expression darkened, his shoulders tensing. "Paris is off-limits. Classified operation. If you're not part of it, you don't need to know."

Jack leaned forward slightly, his smirk turning glacial. "Maybe we do. Considering the money we're offering."

The operative's eyes narrowed, his tone dropping to a threat. "This isn't just about money. The people behind Paris don't tolerate questions. Neither do I."

THE TENSION SNAPPED like a wire under strain. The operative's hand darted toward the pistol at his side, but Irina was faster. Her silenced shot struck his shoulder, spinning him to the ground with a pained grunt.

Chaos erupted. Guards surged forward, weapons raised, but Jack and Irina moved in perfect synchronization. Jack fired twice, his silenced pistol dropping two guards with surgical precision. Irina pivoted, disarming another assailant with a swift kick before taking him down with a clean shot.

"Move!" Jack barked, grabbing the blueprints from the table and shoving them into his bag.

Irina nodded, her pistol raised as she covered their retreat. Gunfire erupted around them, sharp cracks punctuating the din of shouts and scuffling feet. Navigating the maze of tables and crates, they wove through the chaos with unerring precision.

THE FRIGID NIGHT air hit them like a slap as they burst from the warehouse. Shouts echoed behind them, but they sprinted toward their waiting car, their breaths visible in the frigid air.

Jack slid into the driver's seat, the engine roaring to life as Irina climbed in beside him.

"Got what we need?" she asked, her voice steady despite the adrenaline coursing through her veins.

Jack tossed the stolen blueprints onto her lap, his smirk faint but triumphant. "Enough to make some noise."

Irina scanned the documents quickly, her expression hardening. "This isn't just Paris. They're coordinating strikes on transportation hubs across Europe. This is bigger than we thought."

Jack's jaw tightened as he guided the car onto the main road, the city lights blurring past. "Then we hit them where it hurts. No more waiting."

Irina's green eyes stayed on the horizon, her voice cold but resolute. "No more waiting."

AS PRAGUE'S industrial district receded in the rearview mirror, the weight of their discovery pressed heavily between them. The blueprints they'd taken held the key to dismantling The Veil's operations, but the cost of their mission was growing with every step.

And with every confrontation, the line between ally and enemy blurred further, forcing them to question how much of themselves they were willing to sacrifice for victory.

CHAPTER 6
AMBUSHED IN PARIS

PARIS SHIMMERED UNDER A PALE MOON, its timeless beauty masking the growing shadow of danger that crept through its veins. On the roof of a mid-rise building overlooking the Seine, Jack Jones and Irina Stepanov crouched in the biting cold, their breaths visible in the frigid night air. Below them, tucked into the industrial outskirts, lay their target: a gray, unassuming water treatment facility.

By day, it supplied clean water to millions of Parisians. Tonight, it was the staging ground for The Veil's next attack.

"They're using the main reservoir to deliver the payload," Irina murmured, her green eyes fixed on the loading dock below. Trucks moved in and out, their motions purposeful, while guards patrolled the perimeter with practiced efficiency.

Jack adjusted the suppressor on his pistol, his sharp blue eyes narrowing as he assessed the operation. "Which means we don't have much time. Once they load it, it's over."

Irina's gaze didn't waver. "Then let's make sure it doesn't leave."

THE INFILTRATION WAS silent and swift. Jack and Irina moved through the shadows like ghosts, slipping past cameras and weaving between parked trucks. The faint hum of machinery filled the air, punctuated by the occasional murmur of guards trading low conversations.

They reached the loading bay, where workers were unloading crates marked with biohazard symbols. Jack crouched behind a stack of pallets, his pistol steady in his grip. He scanned the scene with precision, taking in every detail.

"They're prepping the dispersal unit," he whispered into his mic. "Almost done."

Irina's voice crackled softly in his ear. "I'll handle the workers. You neutralize the unit."

Jack smirked faintly. "You always get the fun jobs."

IRINA MOVED FIRST, her steps silent but deliberate. She approached the workers with lethal efficiency, her silenced pistol rising as she fired the first shot. The worker crumpled before he could react, while a swift kick to another's knee sent him sprawling. When the last worker fumbled for his radio, her second shot dropped him before he could make a sound.

"Clear," she said, her voice calm, as if the violence had left no ripple in her composure.

Jack moved toward the dispersal unit, a sleek, cylindrical device that exuded an air of menace. Its digital display blinked ominously, counting down with cold precision. He knelt beside it, pulling out his multitool.

"Clock's ticking," Jack muttered, his fingers steady as they began dismantling the complex trigger mechanism.

THE SOUND of heavy boots echoed down the corridor. Irina turned sharply, her green eyes narrowing as a team of heavily armed guards appeared, their weapons raised.

"We've got company," she warned, moving to cover behind a stack of crates.

Jack didn't look up, his focus locked on the dispersal unit. "Keep them busy. I need two minutes."

Irina's pistol barked softly, her controlled bursts precise. The first guard fell with a muffled grunt, his chest blooming red. The second fired back, his bullets sparking off the metal walls, forcing Irina to duck. She reloaded smoothly, firing again and dropping him mid-step.

"Two minutes is a long time," she muttered, her voice edged with dry irritation.

Jack smirked faintly, his gaze never leaving the device. "You'll manage."

THE FIRST EXPLOSION rocked the facility, a deafening boom that sent shockwaves through the structure. Dust rained from the ceiling as alarms blared, the air thickening with smoke.

"That wasn't me," Jack said, glancing up.

Irina's voice was sharp. "They're covering their tracks—destroying the evidence. We need to move, now."

Jack's hands worked faster, dismantling the primary trigger and halting the countdown. The dispersal unit powered down, its ominous hum fading.

"It's neutralized, but not destroyed," Jack said, slinging the device over his shoulder. "We'll finish the job later. Let's go."

THEIR ESCAPE WAS CHAOS INCARNATE. Flames licked at the facility's walls, the acrid scent of burning chemicals stinging their noses. Guards scrambled to contain the destruction, their shouts lost in the cacophony of alarms and secondary explosions.

Jack and Irina moved with precision, weaving through smoke-filled corridors toward the loading dock. They burst into the open air just as a truck screeched to a halt in front of them.

The driver leapt from the cab, his rifle raised, but Jack's silenced shot dropped him before he could fire.

"Get in," Jack barked, motioning to the vehicle.

Irina climbed into the passenger seat, her pistol still drawn as Jack slid behind the wheel. The engine roared to life, the truck lurching forward as they sped away from the inferno behind them.

THE QUIET OF the open road was a stark contrast to the chaos they'd just escaped. Jack drove with steady hands, his sharp blue eyes fixed on the horizon. Beside him, Irina scanned the darkness for signs of pursuit, her green eyes hard and unyielding.

"We stopped the payload," Jack said finally, breaking the silence.

Irina's gaze flicked toward him, her expression grim. "For now. But this wasn't just about Paris. They're testing us—seeing how far we'll go to stop them."

Jack smirked faintly, though it didn't reach his eyes. "Then let's show them."

Their destination was a safe house on the outskirts of the city, a modest apartment tucked into a quiet residential block. Jack parked the truck in an alley, his movements quick and deliberate as he stepped out.

Inside, they secured the dispersal unit in a reinforced case, its sleek menace a reminder of the stakes they faced. Irina opened her laptop, her fingers moving rapidly over the keyboard.

"We need to decode the data stored in this thing," she said. "If it's part of a larger plan, it'll tell us where to go next."

Jack leaned against the wall, his jaw tightening. "And if it doesn't?"

Irina's green eyes met his, her voice steady. "Then we make them tell us."

OUTSIDE, rain began to fall, its steady rhythm a stark counterpoint to the chaos they'd left behind. Jack stood by the window, his sharp gaze fixed on the glimmering city lights in the distance.

"We're running out of time," he whispered.

Irina's voice was soft but firm. "Then we don't waste any of it."

The room fell silent as they turned their focus to the next step. The Veil was closing in, but Jack and Irina had faced long odds before.

This time, they would push back harder than ever.

CHAPTER 7
THE FINAL GAMBIT

THE LONDON SKYLINE GLEAMED in the early evening, a study in shadow and light. Iconic landmarks stood like sentinels against a deepening twilight, their elegance hiding the growing storm below. Jack Jones and Irina Stepanov had no time to admire the view. From the shadows of a Canary Wharf alleyway, they studied their target: a sleek, glass-paneled skyscraper housing The Veil's nerve center.

"This is it," Irina murmured, her green eyes sharp behind the binoculars. The faint glow of her tablet reflected off her face as she scrolled through the stolen data from Paris. "Volkov's command hub. If we're right, every piece of their operation funnels through this building."

Jack adjusted the strap of his tactical vest, his sharp blue eyes narrowing. "Top floors. That's where he's running the show. Take him out, expose the data, and this whole network falls apart."

Irina lowered the binoculars, her voice edged with steel. "And if we're wrong?"

Jack smirked faintly, though the weight in his voice betrayed his unease. "We're not wrong. Let's finish this."

THE SKYSCRAPER'S lobby was a temple of modern luxury. Marble floors gleamed under soft lighting, and minimalist sculptures flanked the walls, their abstract forms casting distorted shadows. But behind the polished veneer, the tension was palpable: plainclothes guards lingered near the reception desk, their postures too deliberate to be casual. Surveillance cameras tracked every angle, and locked elevators hinted at layers of hidden security.

Jack and Irina slipped in through a side door, merging with a small group of employees leaving for the night. Jack's easy demeanor masked the sharp awareness coiled beneath the surface. Irina followed a step behind, her sharp gaze flicking to exits and potential threats.

At the elevator bank, Irina brushed past a distracted guard, her deft hand swiping his access card. She handed it to Jack without missing a beat.

"Top floor," she murmured.

Jack inserted the card and pressed the button, his sharp blue eyes fixed on the glowing numbers as the elevator began its ascent. The faint hum of machinery filled the silence.

"No turning back now," Jack said.

Irina smirked faintly. "We passed that point a long time ago."

THE TOP FLOOR was a fortress of glass, steel, and cutting-edge technology. Offices with glass walls surrounded a sprawling command center, where glowing monitors displayed live feeds from across the globe. Tactical overlays mapped operations in progress, while streams of data scrolled across the screens, revealing the breadth of The Veil's influence.

And at the center of it all was Ambassador Elias Volkov.

Volkov's silver hair gleamed under the harsh lights, his posture composed and commanding as he issued orders to a cluster of operatives. His voice carried the quiet authority of a man accustomed to obedience.

"Berlin and Rome are secured," Volkov said, his tone calm but resolute. "Paris requires more oversight. The public must see chaos, but it must be *our* chaos. No mistakes."

From the shadows, Jack and Irina observed the scene. Jack's jaw tightened, his pistol steady in his grip.

"I've got the servers," Irina whispered, nodding toward a row of computers humming along one wall. "I'll extract the data and plant the virus. You deal with Volkov."

Jack's smirk returned, faint and sharp. "You always give me the fun jobs."

———

IRINA SLIPPED AWAY, her movements precise as she reached the servers. Connecting her tablet, she initiated the data extraction. Lines of code cascaded across her screen, the faint hum of the machines masking her keystrokes.

Meanwhile, Jack crept closer to Volkov, his sharp blue eyes fixed on the man at the heart of The Veil. Volkov's calm, measured tone carried through the room, his words weaving a narrative of control and inevitability.

Jack stepped into the light, his silenced pistol aimed squarely at Volkov's chest. "End of the line, Volkov."

The room froze. Operatives turned toward Jack, their hands instinctively moving toward concealed weapons. But Volkov raised a hand, his expression betraying only mild interest.

"Mr. Jones," Volkov said, his voice tinged with amusement. "I've been expecting you. I assume this is the part where you deliver a dramatic monologue about justice and retribution?"

Jack smirked faintly. "Thought I'd skip to the part where you lose."

Volkov's eyes narrowed, though his calm demeanor didn't waver. "You're playing a small game, Mr. Jones. Killing me won't stop this. The Veil isn't one man—it's an idea. A new order, inevitable and unstoppable."

Jack's pistol didn't waver. "Save it. You're done."

The first shot shattered the silence. One of Volkov's operatives fired, but Jack dropped to the floor, his return fire striking true. Chaos erupted. Irina's voice crackled through his earpiece, sharp and urgent.

"I'm almost done. Hold them off."

Jack fired again, his movements swift and deliberate as he sought cover behind a steel column. "Working on it," he muttered, sending two more operatives to the ground.

Volkov retreated toward a secured office, his steps quick despite his age. Jack pursued, weaving through the chaos with unrelenting focus.

In the server room, Irina completed the transfer, the screen flashing green as her virus began dismantling The Veil's network. She disconnected her tablet, her pistol already in hand as she moved to rejoin Jack.

"Data's ours," she said into her mic. "Their system's crashing as we speak."

"Perfect timing," Jack replied, his voice strained. "Volkov's trying to make a run for it."

THE FINAL CONFRONTATION unfolded in Volkov's private office. Sparse but elegant, the room was dominated by floor-to-ceiling windows offering a breathtaking view of the London skyline. Volkov stood near the desk, his hands raised in mock surrender, his composure unshaken despite the blood staining his sleeve.

"You've won this round, Mr. Jones," Volkov said, his voice calm. "But you're smart enough to know this doesn't end with me. Kill me, and another will take my place. Power is perpetual."

Jack tilted his head, his smirk cold. "Then I'll make sure the next guy knows what's waiting for him."

Volkov's gaze flicked toward the window behind Jack, and in that split second, he lunged for a concealed weapon beneath his desk.

Jack fired first. The silenced shot was precise. Volkov collapsed, his blood pooling on the pristine carpet.

Irina entered moments later, her green eyes sweeping the scene. "It's done?"

Jack nodded, his blue eyes hard. "It's done."

THEIR ESCAPE WAS as chaotic as their infiltration. Alarms blared, and armed guards flooded the building, but Jack and Irina moved with lethal precision. By the time they reached the street, the building's lights were flickering, a sign that Irina's virus had done its job.

As they climbed into their waiting car, Jack glanced at Irina. "We just dismantled the biggest criminal network in the world."

Irina smirked faintly, though her green eyes remained watchful. "And painted targets on our backs."

Jack started the engine, his smirk returning. "Wouldn't have it any other way."

The car roared into the night, leaving the skyscraper and The Veil's crumbling empire in their wake.

CHAPTER 8
THE PRICE OF FREEDOM

THE SAFE HOUSE on the outskirts of London was a far cry from their usual temporary refuges. Hidden behind a row of derelict warehouses, the nondescript building blended into the urban decay. Inside, the faint orange glow of streetlights seeped through the curtains, casting long shadows across the small table where Jack Jones and Irina Stepanov sat.

Between them lay the stolen data drive—a simple, unassuming piece of hardware that held the key to dismantling The Veil's global network. The mission to secure it had been a victory on paper, but the weight in the room suggested otherwise.

Jack leaned back in his chair, his sharp blue eyes fixed on the drive. "We've gutted their infrastructure, exposed their plans, and sent their lieutenants scrambling. But it's not over, is it?"

Irina met his gaze, her green eyes cold. "Not even close. Volkov's death was a blow, but his people won't vanish. They'll regroup, take their operations deeper underground. This is only the beginning."

Jack's smirk was faint, laced with bitterness. "Good to know we're still VIPs in this nightmare."

The air grew heavier as they pored over the final pieces of intel Irina had extracted. The files were damning—bank records, encrypted communications, and blueprints for future operations. The names of influential backers stood out like a poison running through the veins of governments and corporations.

"This could topple entire regimes," Irina murmured, scrolling through the data. "If we release this, it won't just be The Veil that falls. The fallout could cripple global systems."

Jack's jaw tightened, his voice low. "Maybe they deserve to fall."

Irina's gaze snapped to him, her tone sharp. "And what about the millions caught in the collapse? The ones who don't even know this war exists?"

Jack sighed, rubbing his face. "So what's the play? Hand this over to the same agencies trying to kill us? Leak it to the press and watch the world burn?"

Irina's fingers brushed the edge of the drive. "We need allies. People who can act on this without turning it into another power grab."

"People like Gray?" Jack asked, sarcasm edging his tone.

Irina didn't flinch. "Someone like him. Someone who hasn't revealed their hand yet."

The faint hum of an approaching engine interrupted their debate. Jack's sharp eyes flicked to the window, his hand moving instinctively to his pistol.

"We expecting company?" he murmured.

Irina was already on her feet, her silenced weapon drawn. "Not the friendly kind."

Headlights cut through the darkness as a black SUV rolled to a stop outside the safe house. Its engine idled, the faint glow of the interior light revealing two figures inside, their faces obscured by tinted windows.

Jack moved to the doorway, tension coiled in his frame. "Let's make this quick."

The knock that followed was sharp and deliberate. Irina stood to the side of the door, her green eyes narrowing as she nodded. Jack opened it cautiously, keeping his pistol raised just out of sight.

A tall, wiry man stepped into the dim light, his hands raised in a gesture of surrender. His tailored suit was damp from the misty London air, but his demeanor radiated calm.

"Mr. Jones. Ms. Stepanov," the man said, his clipped voice betraying an upper-class accent. "I believe we have mutual interests."

Jack's smirk was wary. "Funny. We were just talking about who to trust."

The man's dark eyes flicked to the drive on the table. "You have something the world needs to see. And I have the means to ensure it's used properly."

Irina's green eyes hardened. "And who exactly are you?"

The man offered a faint smile. "Call me Sinclair. Let's just say I represent a group that understands the dangers of unchecked power—whether it's The Veil or the agencies you've left behind."

THE NEGOTIATION WAS TENSE, a test of wills as much as strategy. Sinclair laid out his offer: resources, protection, and the infrastructure to disseminate the intel strategically. The goal was clear—collapse The Veil's network without unleashing chaos on an unsuspecting world.

"You're asking us to trust you with something that could reshape everything," Jack said, his voice hard. "Why should we believe you're different from the people we've been fighting?"

Sinclair's gaze didn't waver. "Because I know what happens when systems collapse unchecked. I've seen it. My group isn't here to seize power—we're here to prevent it from consolidating again."

Irina's expression remained unreadable. "And if we refuse?"

"Then you'll keep running," Sinclair replied smoothly. "And the truth will die in the shadows."

AFTER SINCLAIR LEFT, the room was heavy with unspoken tension. The drive still sat on the table, its significance far greater than its unassuming form suggested.

Jack leaned against the wall, staring at the ceiling. "What do you think?"

Irina sat down, her fingers brushing the edge of the drive. "I think we're out of options. If Sinclair's lying, we'll deal with it. But if he's telling the truth..."

Jack nodded, his smirk faint but resigned. "Then maybe we can finally end this."

LATER THAT NIGHT, rain began to fall in a steady rhythm, its soft patter breaking the silence. Jack and Irina sat on the steps outside the safe house, their breath visible in the cool night air.

"What happens after this?" Jack asked, his voice quiet.

Irina didn't look at him, her green eyes focused on the misty horizon. "We disappear. For good this time."

Jack's smirk was faint, tinged with something bittersweet. "Together?"

Irina's lips curved into the faintest of smiles. "Always."

The rain washed away the tension for a moment, leaving only the quiet bond between them. One final move lay ahead—one last chance to bring The Veil down before the shadows consumed them for good.

CHAPTER 9
ONE LAST BETRAYAL

THE SECLUDED CABIN in the Scottish Highlands stood in stark contrast to the chaos Jack Jones and Irina Stepanov had left behind. Mist rolled over the surrounding hills, clinging to the evergreens like a shroud. The damp air carried the scent of pine and earth, its tranquility a fragile illusion.

Jack stood at the single window, his sharp blue eyes scanning the ridge beyond the cabin. His movements were restless, his posture coiled. "Something feels off. Sinclair was too eager to take the drive."

Irina sat at the small wooden table, methodically cleaning her pistol. Her green eyes flicked up to meet his, a faint smirk tugging at her lips. "You're pacing," she said lightly. "That's usually my thing."

Jack didn't answer immediately, his gaze fixed on the horizon. "You don't build resources like that without strings attached."

Irina set her pistol down, her smirk fading. "And we're the ones they'll yank first."

THE LOW RUMBLE of engines broke the quiet. Irina rose smoothly, crossing to the window. "SUVs," she murmured, her tone clipped. "At least three, coming over the ridge."

Jack grabbed his rifle, his voice hard. "Either they found us, or Sinclair gave them the map."

"They've found us," she said simply.

Jack turned from the window. "Two minutes out, maybe less. Rear exit leads to open ground."

Irina shook her head. "They'll pick us off before we clear the hill."

"Then we hold here." Jack moved to the center of the room, pulling a supply bag closer. "Force them to come to us."

Irina smirked faintly, though her green eyes were sharp. "Wouldn't be the first time we've been double-crossed."

Jack nodded, loading his rifle. "Let's make it the last."

———

THE FIRST SHOTS shattered the cabin's windows, embedding in the thick wooden walls. Jack fired back, the crack of his rifle splitting the air as he picked off two attackers emerging from the lead SUV.

"Multiple hostiles," he called, his voice steady despite the chaos. "Full tactical gear. Kill squad, not cleanup."

Irina dropped behind the table, firing in controlled bursts. Her movements were swift and deliberate, her pistol's silencer muting the sharp precision of her shots. "They're professionals. Someone doesn't want us leaving this valley alive."

Jack ducked as a bullet splintered the doorframe beside him. "Too bad for them," he muttered, reloading.

Smoke and dust filled the air as bullets tore through the cabin, shattering glass and chipping away at the walls. Jack moved to the rear, covering the back entrance as Irina fired on attackers flanking the side.

"They're trying to surround us!" she called, her voice edged with urgency.

Jack shifted position, his rifle barking as he dropped another operative in the doorway. "Not happening. Keep them pinned!"

A sudden explosion rocked the cabin, sending Jack sprawling. His ears rang, the world spinning before he pushed himself up, rifle in hand.

"I'm fine," Irina called, her tone sharp. She emerged from the smoke, favoring cover as she reloaded. "But they've got heavier fire-power. We need to move."

Jack grabbed the supply bag, slinging it over his shoulder. "Forest. We use the trees for cover."

Irina nodded, her green eyes cold. "Let's go."

THE FOREST WAS DENSE, its towering pines casting deep shadows over the damp earth. Mist curled between the trunks, shrouding the pursuit in an eerie silence broken only by the distant sound of engines and shouted commands.

"They're tracking us," Irina said softly, her steps careful despite the uneven ground.

Jack glanced over his shoulder, his sharp blue eyes scanning the dark. "Then we make them regret it."

They moved quickly, using the terrain to their advantage. As the attackers closed in, Jack and Irina circled back, striking from the shadows. Jack fired from a concealed position, his shots clean and precise, while Irina's silenced pistol dropped another before she disappeared into the mist.

The tide began to turn, but the cost was high. Irina stumbled as a bullet grazed her thigh, the sharp pain forcing her to lean against a tree.

Jack was at her side instantly, his expression hard. "You're hit."

"It's nothing," she said through gritted teeth, though her breathing was labored.

Jack helped her to her feet, his tone urgent but steady. "We need to keep moving. They'll regroup."

Irina managed a faint smirk. "So will we."

BY THE TIME they reached the edge of the forest, the attackers had retreated, their losses too heavy to continue. Jack and Irina leaned against a moss-covered boulder, their breaths visible in the freezing air.

"Whoever sent them won't stop," Jack said, his voice low but resolute.

Irina nodded, her green eyes sharp. "Then we make sure they don't get another chance."

Jack glanced at her, his smirk faint but genuine. "Together?"

Irina's lips curved into a tired smile. "Always."

———

THE FIRST LIGHT of dawn crept over the horizon as they reached a hidden trail leading to a waiting vehicle. Jack slid behind the wheel, his sharp blue eyes fixed on the road ahead.

Irina settled into the passenger seat, her leg freshly bandaged, though her posture remained tense. "What now?"

Jack's voice was quiet but unyielding. "We finish this. If Sinclair sold us out, he's first."

Irina's gaze darkened, her tone cold. "And if he didn't?"

Jack's smirk returned, edged with determination. "Then he'd better have answers."

The car disappeared into the misty valley, carrying them toward a reckoning—one that would end their war for good, no matter the cost.

CHAPTER 10
ENDGAME

THE REMOTE ISLAND off the Scottish coast was cloaked in mist, its rocky cliffs battered by relentless waves. Jack Jones and Irina Stepanov crouched near the edge of a dense thicket, their sharp eyes fixed on the fortified compound below.

Built for secrecy, the compound sprawled across the cove like a concrete scar—squat, brutalist buildings surrounded by high fences and patrolled by armed guards. Beyond it, the ocean stretched endlessly, the crash of waves masking the faint hum of generators.

"This is it," Irina murmured, her green eyes steady as she scanned the facility through binoculars. "The Veil's last stronghold. What's left of their leadership is inside."

Jack adjusted the suppressor on his rifle, his sharp blue eyes narrowing. "And Sinclair. If he's alive, he's in there."

Irina smirked faintly, though her tone was serious. "Or dead, if this is another one of his games."

Jack's expression hardened. "We finish this. No more running, no more shadows."

Irina nodded, her voice steady. "Together."

A sudden gust of wind carried the tang of saltwater and the faint rumble of waves. Irina glanced toward the cliffs, her voice low. "The tide's coming in fast."

Jack crouched behind a boulder, his gaze fixed on the compound. "If it rises, our escape route's underwater. We'll have to work fast."

Irina smirked faintly. "No pressure, then."

THE INFILTRATION BEGAN under the cover of darkness. Moving like shadows, Jack and Irina wove through the damp grass and rocky terrain, their movements silent and deliberate. Years of experience had taught them how to slip through even the tightest patrols.

The first guard fell to Jack's swift strike, a single blow rendering him unconscious before he was dragged into the thicket. Irina handled the next, her silenced pistol firing once, the guard crumpling to the ground.

They reached the outer wall of the compound, their synchronization seamless. Irina retrieved a small device from her bag, attaching it to the fence's control panel. A faint click signaled the deactivation of the electrified barrier.

"Clear," she whispered.

Jack nodded, slipping through the gap in the fence. "Let's make this count."

INSIDE, the compound was stark and functional, its cold floodlights throwing sharp shadows over utilitarian buildings. Jack and Irina moved quickly, weaving through alleys and keeping to the cover of supply crates.

"The main building," Jack murmured, nodding toward the largest structure at the center of the compound. Its windows glowed faintly, the light betraying the activity within. "That's where they'll be running operations."

Irina's green eyes flicked to the windows. "And where Sinclair's intel pointed. If he's here, that's where we'll find him."

Jack's jaw tightened. "Let's hope he's not another dead end."

THE MAIN BUILDING'S interior was eerily quiet, its concrete walls illuminated by glowing monitors displaying global feeds. Digital maps, financial graphs, and tactical overlays revealed the remnants of The Veil's reach. The faint hum of servers underpinned the tension in the air.

In the central command room, a group of operatives huddled around a table covered in maps and dossiers. At the head of the table stood Sinclair, his wiry frame composed but tense.

Jack stepped into the room, his silenced pistol trained on Sinclair. "You've got a lot of explaining to do."

The room froze. Operatives reached for their weapons, but Irina's cold voice cut through the tension.

"Don't," she said, her pistol aimed at the nearest operative. "Unless you want to join Volkov."

Sinclair raised his hands slowly, his dark eyes meeting Jack's. "You're here sooner than I expected."

"Funny," Jack replied, his tone icy. "We weren't sure if you'd even be here—or if you'd sent us to die."

Sinclair's lips curved into a faint smile. "If I wanted you dead, you'd be dead. I brought you here to end this."

THE CONFRONTATION WAS RAZOR-SHARP. Sinclair explained that The Veil's leadership had fractured after Volkov's death. He had manipulated events to draw the remaining leaders into one place, creating the perfect opportunity to dismantle the organization for good.

"You're not the only ones fighting this war," Sinclair said, his voice calm but firm. "But it's a war that can't be won with morality alone."

Jack's sharp blue eyes didn't waver. "Spare me the philosophy. If you've got a plan, say it."

Sinclair gestured to the dossiers spread across the table. "Their infrastructure is crumbling, but they still have access to weapons, accounts, and operatives. The only way to ensure they don't rebuild is to take out the leaders—and destroy everything in this compound."

Irina's green eyes narrowed. "And what's stopping you from taking over when it's done?"

Sinclair met her gaze evenly. "You are. Once this is over, I'm gone. No power grabs. Just the satisfaction of watching them burn."

Jack's grip on his pistol relaxed slightly. "Then let's get to work."

THE COMPOUND ERUPTED INTO CHAOS. Jack and Irina moved with precision, their weapons clearing hallways and eliminating resistance. Bullets ricocheted off concrete walls as smoke and shouting filled the air.

Jack's rifle barked in controlled bursts, each shot precise as he cleared rooms and neutralized threats. Irina moved like a shadow, her silenced pistol dropping attackers before they could react.

In the command room, Sinclair worked feverishly to overload the servers. His fingers flew across the keyboard, alarms blaring as the system's self-destruct sequence activated. "Once this goes up, everything they've built disappears," he said.

"Just make sure you're clear before it does," Jack called over his shoulder, covering the door.

The climax came in the lower levels, where the remaining leaders made their stand. The firefight was brutal, with Jack and Irina moving as one, their synchronization honed by years of survival.

The last shot echoed through the compound, leaving only silence in its wake. Jack and Irina stood amidst the wreckage, their breaths heavy but steady.

"It's done," Jack said, his voice quiet.

Irina nodded, her green eyes hard. "Let's get out before we go with it."

THE EXPLOSION ROCKED the island as they sped away in a stolen boat, flames consuming the compound and lighting up the night sky. The shockwave rippled across the water, sending tremors through the small craft.

Jack stood at the helm, the cold wind whipping through his hair, while Irina sat beside him, her gaze fixed on the horizon.

"No more Veil," Jack said, his voice quiet but resolute.

Irina smirked faintly. "And no more us, either. At least not in this world."

Jack glanced at her, his smirk softening into something genuine. "Together?"

Irina's smile was faint but real. "Always."

As the island disappeared behind them, the weight of their mission lifted, leaving them with a rare, fleeting sense of freedom. The war was over, but the future was unwritten—and, for the first time, it was theirs to decide.

EPILOGUE

THE SMALL COASTAL village felt like a world away from the chaos Jack Jones and Irina Stepanov had left behind. Nestled along the rocky shores of an unnamed island, its whitewashed cottages and narrow cobblestone streets exuded a quiet simplicity. The salty tang of the ocean hung in the air, carried by a gentle breeze that whispered of calm seas and forgotten struggles.

Jack leaned against the railing of a weathered dock, his sharp blue eyes fixed on the horizon. The faint hum of a fishing boat reached his ears, mingling with the distant cries of seagulls. His stance was relaxed, but the ever-present edge in his demeanor hadn't completely faded.

Behind him, Irina's boots crunched softly against the planks. She carried two steaming cups of coffee, her faint smile a rare but familiar sight. "Still watching for enemies?" she teased, her green eyes glinting as she handed him a cup.

Jack smirked faintly, taking the coffee but keeping his gaze on the waves. "Old habits die hard."

"Not a bad habit to have," Irina said, leaning against the railing beside him. "Keeps us alive."

Jack sipped his coffee, the warmth cutting through the morning chill. "If anyone's left to come after us, they'll have to work for it. We've done enough running."

Irina turned her gaze to him, her smirk subtle but knowing. "Think you can live like this? Quiet days, no explosions?"

Jack chuckled softly, surprising her. "Might take some getting used to. You?"

Irina's green eyes followed the rhythm of the waves, her voice contemplative. "I think I could try. No agencies. No missions. No Veil. Just... quiet."

The dock creaked beneath them as they stood shoulder to shoulder, letting the silence settle. For a fleeting moment, the weight of their shared past seemed to dissolve into the ocean's gentle cadence.

MILES AWAY, in a city neither of them would return to, a dimly lit office buzzed with quiet activity. A man sat at a desk cluttered with documents and photographs, his crisp suit unmarred by the chaos he orchestrated.

The soft glow of a desk lamp illuminated a dossier bearing a familiar emblem: **The Veil.** Grainy photos of Jack and Irina lay scattered among pages of operational notes and surveillance reports.

The man leaned back in his chair, his dark eyes glinting as he picked up one of the photos, studying it with a cold smile. "They think it's over," he murmured.

With deliberate precision, he closed the file, locking it inside a drawer before rising. His silhouette was framed by the window, the sprawling cityscape stretching out below him like a chessboard.

The faint trill of a phone cut through the stillness. He answered it without hesitation, his voice calm and commanding.

"Activate the next phase."

BACK ON THE DOCK, the morning light began to break over the horizon, casting golden hues across the water. Jack leaned on the railing, his gaze distant.

"Quiet's nice," he said softly, his smirk fading into a thoughtful frown. "But it doesn't last long. Not for people like us."

Irina's green eyes didn't waver from the waves. "If it comes, we'll deal with it. But for now, we've earned this."

Jack nodded, his smirk returning, softer this time. "For now."

The waves lapped gently against the dock as the first rays of sunlight warmed their faces. Together, they faced the horizon, knowing the future was unwritten—and no matter what lay ahead, they would meet it as they always had: side by side.

Miles away, the shadowed figure in the office smiled coldly, flipping through the dossier one last time. His voice was barely a whisper, but his intent was unmistakable.

"They'll be back."

On the dock, the quiet persisted, but the air carried the faint, unshakable tension of a storm waiting to break. For now, Jack and Irina stood at the edge of a new chapter, one they would write together, no matter who—or what—tried to stop them.

The End

Did you enjoy *Agents of Deception*?

Please consider reviewing it on Goodreads, Bookbub or your favorite retailer. Reviews help me reach new readers.

If you would like to read more stories featuring Jack and Irina, **join my newsletter and let me know!**

Meanwhile, have you read the ***Retired Assassins' Club*** or the ***City of Lies*** series?

ABOUT THE AUTHOR

Sam Chase delivers heart-pounding thrillers crafted for quick reads. Whether you're commuting, relaxing, or need a break, these stories will keep you on the edge of your seat.

Website: www.samchaseauthor.com

Newsletter: samchaseauthor.substack.com

𝕏 x.com/samchaseauthor

🅰 amazon.com/author/samchasemystery

BB bookbub.com/authors/sam-chase-0987d23f-73d9-4b97-9954-5f9fce0c0ce3

🅖 goodreads.com/samchaseauthor

ALSO BY SAM CHASE

Retired Assassins' Club

The Scholar

The Widow

The Locksmith

The Cost

The Conductor

Agents of Deception

Alliance

Shadow Pursuit

Double Crossed

Deep Cover

Endgame

City of Lies

Hunted

Fractured

Veiled

Marked

Exposed